MY EYES FLUTTERED OPEN TO DARKNESS, but I didn't need to see my surroundings to know where I was. Even after years of sitting mired in the muck, abandoned by her crew, the antiseptic smell of a medical bay lingered—that, or the *Rapscallion* owners had pumped in the unmistakable aroma for the tourists.

"Cain?" I struggled to sit up but couldn't—not from a lack of physical ability but because of the restraints covering my body.

I screamed, bloodcurdlingly fearful and furious. Small spaces aren't great for me. The hab-unit on the *Starshine* barely passed acceptable levels. At least in that cramped space, I had room to move, even if only a few steps in either direction. I couldn't stand being strapped down and forcibly restricted. I was about to go into a full-blown panic attack if something didn't change within the next few seconds.

Nothing changed.

THE RAPSCALLION

THE THREE-FOLD SUNS

Book 1

by

ELIZABETH KNOLLSTON

LEWIS BROS PRESS

ISBN Paperback: 978-1-959159-00-1
ISBN Ebook: 978-1-959159-01-8

Cover Art and Interior Design © Elizabeth Knollston
Editing by Red Adept Editing Services

Published by Lewis Bros. Press
PO Box 261
Larned, KS 67550

visit www.elizabethknollston.com

for my mom and dad who nurtured
my love of stories
this first book is for you

1

TricLath Pudding

The extravagant buffet sat waiting for some unsuspecting fool to dive right in. I eyeballed the vibrant colors laced with tantalizing olfactory stimulants, all crafted to trigger memories unique to each passerby. The buffet was a mouthwatering spread, the food crying out for a dessert of antinausea and other preventative digestive medications.

Don't get me wrong. I loved most of the food, all artfully plated and arranged. I'm just not keen on the chef, a jolly Jip by the name of Juff. Look, cultural traditions and belief systems are a hobby of mine. Picked it up from my pops, who studied with the top-notch xenologists of his day, Dr. Emri Doubi and Dr. Si-Ial Ashter. Both were famous individuals, now cited in a myriad of textbooks.

Pops believed in hard work. He never subscribed to what he called armchair xenos, students or academics who latched onto the latest trends sporting remote operations. Sending robotic and artificial intelligence drones to dig sites or planets to collect information was all well and good for follow-up research, but Pops believed in getting his hands dirty, especially when breaking ground on a new site.

With his philosophy decidedly entrenched, Pops dragged my brother and me right along with him on his travels. My childhood consisted of being out in the elements, digging in the soil, stumbling through ruins, and listening to Pops's stories. If not for the Cricade Wars, I firmly believe Pops's name would be cited right along with Doubi and Ashter.

Ever heard of Epo-5? Yeah, I thought so. We spent almost an entire year on that miserable planet. Pops believed it held some great galactic secret. I tell you, mucking around in waste bogs was not my idea of creative education.

Right. Wormhole. Sorry, the tendency to ramble runs in the family.

The Jip chef. Fascinating species, for sure. An intricate culture steeped in the arts and spirituality. But all those little flecks of spice are sanctified dirt. That's right—dirt. In order for it to be sanctified, the dirt is taken from the soles of their Holy Travelers. Jip biology boasts cast-iron stomachs. They can eat anything— literally anything. As a human who can't afford basic bioupgrades, I'm a little more discerning.

My stomach growled because the smells wafting from the table weren't enough to fill my belly. Fu... fudge nuggets.

Sorry. Not the food—although they do sound kind of appetizing... "Fudge nuggets" as in I'm working really hard at cleaning up my language. Not that it matters this far out from Earth, away from the ever-present ears of my Wepli bosses.

How that species ever became entangled with humanity's messy, complicated, and often ridiculous language extensions is beyond my understanding. Their language is to the point and compact. But hey, Confore Tech signs off on my credit allotment.

Not to mention the fact I earned this awesome voucher for a vacation with, wait... hold on... I've got to check the ticket stub again. Hub Station 7.6... No, that's where I boarded. Mahia... No, that's my name. Oh, right. Desmo Voro Starshine Adventures, onboard their flagship, the *Starshine*. It's one of those best-kept secrets. No one knew about the company because no one but saps like me who redeem their vouchers ever goes on one of their cruises.

Not that I could afford anything else... or even this one. But hey, at least it's a vacation, right? Even if it's an unusual gesture of recognition from a species that believes in hard work for the sake of hard work. I didn't become the help desk hotline aficionado by twiddling my thumbs all day.

As I moved down the buffet line, I spied a third-gen Happy Times vending machine. Thank you, Desmo Voro Starshine Adventures. At least someone had a smart head on their shoulders. Or perhaps even two.

I scanned the projected menu—limited choices, but thank Saturn's rings, all edible. As I punched in the codes for an old-fashioned, honest-to-goodness cheeseburger and fries, the vending machine tagged the HalfLife v-7.91 biochip in my palm—nifty piece of tech for real-time medical information, transfer of credits, and criminal records. That is, if you have a criminal record. Which I don't. Well, kind of. But that's something I don't like to talk about.

These Happy Times vending machines, while notorious for repeated breakdowns and lousy circuits, were developed to provide optimal nutrition on long-haul missions. My cheeseburger and fries would be loaded with vit-mins and whatever else the system determined my biochemistry currently needed.

While true long-haul runs were now uncommon, with all the midway stations and refueling ports peppered throughout space, the vending machines were cheap installs, great choices for maintaining a reasonable food budget. Not exotic food by any stretch of the imagination, but it worked.

Ignoring a burning smell wafting from the vending machine, I grabbed my food and headed over to a small and rather neglected viewing port adjacent to the buffet. The seating area, decorated in a garish yellow-orange combo, a color scheme unfortunately found throughout the *Starshine*, was haphazardly arranged in a bulbous extension of the ship. Advert screens, outdated due to the lack of 3-D holographics, scrolled through a myriad of add-ons and buy-ins pushed upon vacationers.

I crossed my fingers and hoped the seating was compliant with space-travel licenses. All commercial space vehicles had to register with ChowHo Insurance Companies. Any added item, chair, table, couch, bed, you name it, had to be secured by either up-to-code grav units or old-school bolts. When the chair wouldn't budge, old school it was.

When I was two bites deep into the cheeseburger, a little old lady took the seat opposite me. We were the only two people eating. She could have chosen a different table—any other table—like the one behind me. That would have been a better choice.

"Having a nice time, dear?"

I chewed slowly. Then I took a long sip of ria bubble tea. Next, I dabbed at my face with a napkin and said, "Sure."

"This is my third trip, but it still feels like my first one each time." The woman speared a piece of meat coated in those flavorful little specks of dirt.

"Uh, I wouldn't if I were you."

The woman winked. "No worries, dear. Had the upgrade after the cruise last year." She took a bite and smiled in pleasure as she chewed.

I pursed my lips, harrumphed, and shrugged. To each their own.

"I can, however, vouch for the TricLath pudding. I must confess I paid the upgrade fees to stock a few of my preferred beverages and foods. I had the TricLath pudding specially imported from Daleron for this trip. Would you care to try mine?"

Despite her polite gesture, I shook my head. "No, thanks. I'm good."

"Please, you must. I insist. What is the fun of a cruise like this without enjoying something of an exotic nature?" The woman leaned forward and pointed at the transparent wrapping covering her dish of pudding. "It's certified fresh… and human grade."

I eyed the delicate mound of cream-colored pudding. It looked scrumptious. I knew about TricLath pudding but hadn't been able to afford a sample as yet. What the heck? The label boasted the imperial stamp of the Old Earth Food Licensing Board. A couple of bites couldn't hurt.

I took the proffered spoon, unwrapped the pudding, and dipped the utensil into the delicacy. As its creamy texture coated my tongue, my mouth exploded with the rich, full flavors of cream, milk, and TricLath-soaked honey.

"It certainly beats the instapuddings. Thanks," I commented unceremoniously around my second mouthful.

The older woman pushed the rest of it my way, and I didn't protest. Hey, if she was willing to share, I wasn't going to stop her. We ate the rest of our food in silence, and when finished, I balled up my trash to throw it into the recycler.

"Did you pay for the premium package?"

Fudge nuggets. I didn't move fast enough. I appreciated her sharing the pudding, but I wasn't into sharing much more than that.

Smiling, I said, "No. My voucher's for the basic tour."

"Oh, a voucher! How lovely! A present?" Wistful memories flashed in her eyes as she added, "My son brings me the best presents."

I'd forgotten how inquisitive other humans could be. Confore Tech consisted of 129 employees, two of which were human, Jorge and me. And Jorge worked three floors above me in the developmental engineering department. That meant I had nothing to do with the only other human at Confore, only that I had spied his name on the company employee roster.

The rest of the employees were Weplies—a hardworking, nose-to-the-grindstone species with little time for chitchat or concern about personal connections. That suited me just fine.

The temptation to walk off was strong. I eyed the recycler box, just ten steps away… Then out the door to freedom.

"No. Won it cause of work. Job well done or something like that." I found my mouth moving of its own accord.

The woman's eyes lit up. "Congratulations! Where do you work?"

I gritted my teeth. "Confore Tech. Help desk."

"A Wepli company. Their logo has two…" The woman paused, frowned, and glanced off to one side, trying to recall what it looked like.

I helped her out. "Two hands with the glowing circuit ball above them."

"Yes, of course. You must have outstanding qualifications then. What schooling branch did you attend?"

But that was all my daily allotted social-courtesy levels could handle.

"If you'll excuse me, I should do some reading before our first outing."

Her face crumpled into a pile of wrinkles, and I felt a stab of guilt. The woman was sporting the drab browns and grays of ill-fitting clothes, paired with a vibrant-green triangular hat—all the latest rage among those wealthy enough to live in Cloud-11. Considering that, combined with her aged appearance and hunched shoulders, I bet she had it all, money and family. In my experience, very few humans made it to the older age bracket without the credits to pay for all the buy-ins required for medical care, let alone life extensions.

Why would she be traveling alone? Least of all on a craptacular cruise ship? Family units stuck together, even more so the higher up one looked in the echelons of humanity's wealthiest.

"Perhaps I'll see you later." The warble in her voice was like a knife to my heart.

Crickets.

"Maybe you could give me the rundown on the outing?" I said. "Since you said you've done these tours before?"

Her brown eyes lit up, and her smile revealed two rows of blindingly white teeth. Yup. Definitely loaded with credits.

"I would be honored," she said.

Pesky social-guilt traps had never bothered me in the past. Why did it now? Who knows? I forced a smile, gathered up her trash with mine, and tossed it into the recycler.

2

Research Your Vacations before Vacationing

I followed the woman reluctantly to the observation deck, a popular choice of the other passengers, much to my chagrin. Taking up the majority of the center was a Glipglow family unit, a reptilian species from the Lower Zyph Atmospheres. Judging by the noticeable lower canines, three of the hatchlings were barely old enough to leave the warmer cribs, while the other... eight—no, nine—showed both lower and upper canines, marking them around two years old, the age when the little chompers cut their teeth on anything and everything. Mental note: steer clear of those guys.

Off to one side stood two veiled figures, backs turned to each other in a defensive posture. Identifying the species under the thick blue cloth was difficult, but the tight weave and vibrant blue easily gave away who—or rather, what—they were: Star Eaters.

The species didn't matter. The group held no rules as to where their followers came from, only that they adhered to their religion's bylaws. Don't ask. I refused to look too deeply into their beliefs after a rampage of fanatics ate through a stadium of hoverball fans.

Yes, you heard right.

Ate. Through. Them.

So much fun.

All in all, that meant I had quite a few individuals to avoid on this wonderful cruise, where we were all jammed into the ship together. Go… me… for redeeming the voucher.

At least the observation deck's amenities made up for the less-than-stellar company. Whatever the CEO of Desmo Voro Starshine Adventures was, at least the company spent money upgrading this part of the ship.

If the other passengers would've just headed off and found somewhere else to loiter, I could've enjoyed spending time there. The view-field was well worth the price of admission, stretching from one end of the room to the other and from floor to ceiling, a brilliant example of the minds behind Confore's technologies.

Confore is the largest tech company around, with the highest rates for product quality and customer service. I take pride in that. I'm a key member of the help desk team. Don't give me that look. Just because I have a low tolerance for in-person social exchange doesn't mean I can't be a shining-star wonder at assisting people with all their tech needs.

Over the phone, of course.

I earned the vacation voucher by ensuring I stayed up-to-date on all the latest gadgets and tech Confore offered, including upgrades, recalls, repair specs—you name it, the whole gambit. I even keep a close eye on our competitor's stuff. I'm that good.

That particular view-field was state of the art. Hadn't been on the market for more than a few months. This generation of view-field tech was one of those adrenaline-junkie inventions. To the naked eye, nothing sits between you and the vast emptiness of space just waiting to gobble you up.

The view-field is a pretty nifty piece of tech, actually. It's five layers thick, standard for nonmilitary-grade tech. Each subsequent layer is a redundant field over the parent field, in case of power fluctuations or failures.

With a tier-one or tier-two failure, a general proceed-at-your-own-risk warning is issued. A tier-three failure gets techs sent out to clear the area and solve the problem before they find themselves on the wrong side of an airlock.

In the case of a catastrophic failure—a major, no-holds-barred, all-the-fields-fail-at-once one—then according to ChowHo Insurance and Confore subparagraphs and legalese, the ship should be outfitted with industry-standard bay doors, rigged up and coded to drop within seconds of field failure, squishing anything and anyone in their way.

My mind wandered through a few terrifying scenarios before I realized the old woman was trying to introduce herself. As annoyance got the better of her cultured etiquette, the woman reached out and tapped my arm.

"Tap" isn't exactly the best word because it wasn't gentle. I'm going to have a bruise there for the next few days. The shock of the so-called tap, plus the brief bloom of pain, was my excuse for letting slip a few unsavory words, and I blushed. I might be slightly antisocial, but it doesn't mean I'm completely oblivious.

"Mrs. Fairhaven Gol."

"Nice to meet you, Mrs. Gol," I said as politely as I could. "I'm Mahia."

I could see her expecting the rest of my name, but she wasn't getting it. No one was unless they wore official badges. Even then, they'd have to scan my chip.

Remember when I said my pops's name would've been cited along with those bigwigs in xenology if it hadn't been for the Cricade Wars? The reason wasn't because he died in the wars or the brutal upheavals afterward. Or even the brief period of famine before the Old Earth monarchy stepped in and helped to right the system. Quite the opposite, in fact.

He... Well, to go ahead and spit it out, he fought against the majority of humanity and their allies. He fought for the Eeri.

So my last name isn't something I just blurt out to strangers. It's the main reason I work for Confore. Weplies just don't care. All they care about is their profit-and-loss statements.

I know. Why not go through the courts and change the thing? I tried that.

First off, legally changing your name costs a small planet's worth of credits to finalize the process, and second, the advocate assigned to my case hated me for some odd reason. We'll skip the whole story of how that meet-and-greet went.

"So," I drew the word out, looking to change the

subject, and turned toward the view-field. "What's up with this first outing or excursion or whatever they call it? You've been, right? A starbase or something?"

Last-name questions forgotten, Mrs. Gol dove right in. "Starbase 9.2, formally known as Kel Station. First built in '91 through the partnership of the Goldsmith Consortium, the Telt, and the trade branch of the Eeri."

I couldn't help but cringe at the mention of those cloud suckers.

"The starbase was a focal point for refueling and trade and neutral ground for conflict management until the Brushe Conflict, the inciting incident of the Cricade Wars."

Another cringe. Should've done my homework. Not really keen on hearing any more or walking where those things had been.

I'm all for tolerance and peace and understanding the differences between species, but after what happened, let's just say if a vote arose for blackballing the Eeri, I'm all in. Not that we're playing nice with them right now. Humanity's military eventually pushed them back to their own region of space, but the whispers currently circulating speculate that our current flop-headed government is eyeballing a new treaty.

"And what does this outing entail?"

Mrs. Gol gave me a not so ladylike side-eye and harrumphed at the rude interruption of her tour guide impression. "We get a few hours to wander through the starbase. Basic tourist vendors set up, plus a couple of commercial spaces are there to look at too." All annoyance vanished as she turned and winked. "But save your credits. It's the next stop where you'll find the good stuff."

"What's that?"

"The *Rapscallion*."

Jupiter's moons.

I decided I might have to eat off the buffet for supper. That would've given me a legitimate excuse to miss out on those little outings.

"Take a look at that," Mrs. Gol whispered.

I didn't want to, but I did.

A few more passengers showed their faces. A young human couple was there with two small children—or, should I say, two very bored-looking kids itching to cause trouble.

And a man.

He was more than a man if I'm any judge of exterior appearances. His basic features leaned toward human, but his ash-colored hair, paired with a very noticeable feline tail, meant he had Darquet blood. He didn't have the brow ridge or cranial protrusions a fifty-fifty mix would sport, so I'm guessing a grandparent or maybe even a great-grandparent was full-blooded Darquet.

"What would someone like him be doing here?"

I turned in shock at the acid dripping from Mrs. Gol's words. I hadn't pegged her for a purist, certainly not if she'd taken this cruise a few times before. Purists tended to stick to Old Earth or human-only enclaves. Purist ideology entertained different levels of belief. Most recognized how humanity was irrevocably linked with intergalactic trade routes. Purist politics supported trade agreements and business deals as long as those contracts stipulated humans maintained their own human-only zones. But interbreeding or living amongst different species—nope, that was a strict no go. To put it quite plainly, they were old-fashioned bigots.

I high-fived myself for not giving in to her lonely old-lady wiles and telling her my last name. If Mrs. Gol was indeed a purist, my surname would be on a kill list for sure. Not that she would place in my list of top-ten assassins, but stranger things have happened.

I watched the man.

Don't judge.

He was certainly fit and healthy, his broad chest and well-muscled arms and legs neatly showcased in his choice of formal attire. He was around my age unless he was sporting life extensions—not a common practice, but they were still sold on the open market. It would be a lie to say I considered walking over and introducing myself just to test Mrs. Gol's reaction.

But the old lady grabbed my arm and dragged me to one side. I kid you not. She literally dragged me across the room. I revised my previous assessment and word choice to describe her.

"Gene filth. His ticket should have been disallowed. I'll have to ping the captain and give him an earful." She spat venom while absentmindedly patting my arm.

I chewed on a few retorts but decided against them. Causing a scene or upsetting Mrs. Gol would only bring unwanted attention.

I didn't want to, but I asked, "So, you started to tell me I needed to save my credits for the *Rapscallion*."

Mrs. Gol's eyes darted between me and the man.

She huffed a few times before deciding that showing off her knowledge was preferable to complaining about the company. "Right. Yes."

She motioned me over to one of the benches, and we sat. I half listened to her patter on about a ship I was all too familiar with. It took some effort, but I felt like I managed to keep an eye on the man while maintaining the facade of paying attention to her, enough so that my internal musings got snagged.

"Sorry," I said. "Can you repeat that?"

Mrs. Gol blinked. "Of course. I was talking about the upgrades to the *Rapscallion*'s tour. I'm told they've added in some holographic sims, all sourced from the ship's internal recordings and eyewitness testimony. The whole experience should be riveting."

I blanched. "Riveting" wouldn't have been my chosen descriptor. "Revolting" was a better word choice.

"Honored guests of the Desmo Voro Starshine Adventures Cruise Company, we are pleased to announce docking protocols with Starbase 9.2 will commence momentarily. Please queue up in the transfer hub and get ready to explore the first of several eye-opening and stunning stops along our journey." The soothing baritone voice clicked off, and a monotone AI voice reciting the grocery list of terms-of-service agreements switched on.

"If you'll pardon me, I need to grab a few things from my quarters. Shall I see you at the transfer hub?" Mrs. Gol flashed me her most hopeful smile.

I swallowed and, against my better judgment, nodded. "Sure. Wouldn't miss it." I desperately wanted to tag a few more words onto that simple statement, but I kept my mouth shut.

She patted my arm once more before rising and tottering off to the internal parts of the ship reserved for hab-units. I didn't need anything. I didn't want anything but to get off that blasted cruise.

3

Unexpected Thunder and Pesky Do-Gooders

Hours later, after the excursion to the delightfully mind-numbing Starbase 9.2, I managed to shake free of Mrs. Gol and head to my hab-unit. After several hours with the well-intentioned woman, my nerves were shot.

"Excuse me."

The voice sounded like soft, rolling waves of thunder. The simple phrase, rough and full of depth, echoed off the walls of the narrow hallway. I jumped at the unexpected intrusion on my solitude.

I turned to face the speaker and inwardly cringed at allowing my little-old-lady-fueled exhaustion to dampen my awareness of who and what was around me. All I wanted was peace and quiet after the cacophony of enthusiastic tourists unleashed on unscrupulous vendors.

It was the man.

I turned to face him.

Up close, he impressed even more. Stubble peppered his lower jaw and curved around his lips. Ashen hair swept back toward his left temple and tapered down into a buzz around the nape of his neck. Irises of liquid violet watched me study him.

A dream situation—caught in tight quarters with an individual worthy enough of drool.

"Right, yeah. Sorry." My voice cracked, and I tripped over my own stupid feet as I flattened myself against the wall.

The man frowned but nodded and brushed past me, his tail darting back and forth in frustration.

"Way to go, ace," I muttered.

The Wepli work ethic translated into twelve-hour shifts, six days a week. That dictated that my one day off consisted of sleeping or studying the latest tech updates—not an environment conducive to meeting anyone. But that wasn't high on my to-do list either. Keeping my nose clean and out of trouble was more important than random hook-ups.

I tried not to but couldn't help but notice his hab-unit was just three doors down, opposite side of mine. Either he was a thrifty fellow and didn't want to spend the five hundred forty-nine credits for the luxury-suite upgrade, or he wasn't as well off as his appearance suggested.

My mind wouldn't quiet down as I unlocked my own meager hab-unit, stumbled inside, and ran through a bunch of scenarios I won't repeat in polite company.

The economy hab-units were sparse—no surprises there. Each met the specified standard of five-by-four-meter space, complete with a bunk, a decent enough mattress, a Sur-T Screen with a mediocre operating system, and one low-grade Dash an' Wash station.

I flopped down on the bunk and debated with myself on the likelihood of going insane if I stayed in my room for the rest of the cruise. The chances were good for insanity.

Starbase 9.2 had been underwhelming, and I mean that as someone who went in with zero expectations—minus the nail-biting tube lift with the two Star Eaters.

I'd followed Mrs. Gol as she hit all her favorite spots and made appropriate remarks as she pointed out historical markers. Bless me because I did a remarkable job at keeping my comments on an internal loop only. Some poor soul had posted so-called facts all throughout the starbase. I had extreme difficulty keeping myself from busting up after reading a few of them, then not weeping at the general lack of competency among my fellow galactic inhabitants.

I mean, for crying out loud, the Cricade Wars ended only twenty-one years ago. Recent memory, folks. But watching Mrs. Gol go around and nod after rereading a sign for the hundredth time made me question the sanity of our media corporations. And, honestly, I admired the marketing strategies of the vendors who took advantage of all the poor, unfortunate souls who ate it up.

Case in point: Lieutenant Commander McCracken. Yes, that's the man's name. A less-than-stellar officer amongst humanity's military ranks, he was frequently lauded as a military hero. I've read my fair share of cutting-edge news reports, follow-up infographics, and tell-all press junkets from several sources who all carry varying degrees of admiration and disgust for not only McCracken but also several of the names lifted up by the military and megacorporations as heroes from the Cricade Wars.

Everyone agrees on one thing. Lieutenant Commander McCracken was well intentioned but on the clumsy side. How he managed to continue to pass competency tests was beyond my knowledge, and he was reported to have frequently been posted on out-of-the-way, no-action-seeing ships or bases—like Starbase 9.2, erroneously believed to have been safely beyond the war zone.

Several members of the command crew have spoken out against McCracken's rise to fame despite the blackballing of their names and careers and even a few death threats. That leads me to believe them when they all say McCracken tripped while he told a joke, spilled his coffee, and shorted out the weapon controls.

Despite those testimonies and sworn oaths, the media continues to uphold Lt. Commander McCracken for his brilliance in saving Starbase 9.2 with a preemptive attack against the Eeri. Which story do you think the commercial bigwigs of the starbase subscribe to?

You guessed it. On the main floor was a statue dedicated to this war hero who—I have come to believe—was no more than a man who spilled his coffee, which curdled the weapons' command codes and caused a statistically improbable, well-timed strike against the Eeri coming to commandeer the starbase.

But the tourists had been eating up the media's spin on McCracken and shelling out more than a few credits for McCracken dolls for the kiddos—not to mention the little holographic buttons with a serious lieutenant commander looking off into the distance and reciting the resounding words, "Live free or die free."

I know. Gag me.

Tension settled in my shoulders, and I stretched, trying to work loose some of the knots getting too comfortable in my body. Letting out a long sigh, I rolled over onto my side to curl up and take a nap, and something bit my hip.

"Blasted dermatex. I sprang for the extra cleaning fees." I hopped off the bunk and scanned the rumpled sheets.

Those nasty buggers were a gift from the Urminate Clans. The parasites didn't bother the thick-skinned and scaled Urminates but could do damage on tender human flesh. Nothing appeared out of the ordinary, but I stripped back the sheets just to make sure, looking for the telltale rainbow-colored smears indicating dermatex droppings. Nothing.

Annoyed and relieved at the same time, I patted down my jumpsuit, only to be rewarded with another sharp poke. Scowling at the offending object in my pocket, I pulled out a small metal case. Light flashed off its exterior as I flipped the object back and forth, trying to find any identifying markings.

It sure as crickets wasn't mine.

The case appeared bare, with no engravings or encoded watermarks that I could detect. Maybe if I'd gotten the SeeClear 3.5 hardware installation… but I'd declined even though Confore offered to pay for the whole procedure. Despite the one-hundred-percent satisfaction guarantee of no host rejections on bioupgrades,

I'd received an increasing number of calls at the help desk regarding issues customers had experienced. Sometimes, diving into the latest tech before the bugs get worked out isn't such a great idea.

Not to mention how Pops's mentality of rejecting bioupgrades had lodged itself in my own moral compass. The only exception has been the mandatory HalfLife biochips. Their easy-to-access network of information has been hailed as a wonder because the biochips assist emergency services and the InterGalactic Justice system by reducing response times in rendering appropriate aid. When I reached the legal age of eighteen, in a rare haze of buyer's euphoria, I'd opted for the credit transfer upgrade package, making all my purchase dreams a breeze.

I pressed the offending case's trigger latch, and it popped open and revealed a small, nondescript transfer square. Now, any sane person would've left well enough alone, maybe trashed it or reported it. The t-square could've been a con job trying to piggyback off the personal chip network or to insert a virus when plugged into an operating system. Or the random prank of someone looking for extracurricular entertainment. Certainly, anyone who needed to fly under the radar would leave it alone. That was the sensible thing to do.

So I plugged the t-square into the Sur-T Screen, sat down, and waited for it to load.

The standby screen's smiling brunette's face melted into a puddle of goo as the t-square's program asserted itself. The screen fuzzed out then flashed a simple warning: "Stay safe. Danger."

Right, as clear as a Jip's caramel sea-slug pudding.

Hacking wasn't up my alley. I could prattle off the innocuous specs of a TraeC Digger Unit like nobody's business or speed someone through the help files for an UpStart Mobile Patch for bioupgrades, but figuring out if the t-square carried a digital fingerprint or more from this cryptic and nonhelpful message? Nope. Not in my wheelhouse.

Besides, whoever sent me this annoyance should've known I don't like being told what to do. I try hard to follow society's instructions: look both ways before crossing the street, go the extra mile at work, don't splash in Athmio-spawning wading pools, no matter how tempting the iridescent waters look. You know, all the usual things. But it grates on my nerves. Every single time.

What did the message even mean? *"Stay safe. Danger."* I scoffed. If I'd meant to do that, I would have checked the ratings listing for Desmo Voro Starshine Adventures before boarding. I'd already declined the buffet lineup. What could've been more dangerous than that?

You know, that isn't what bothered me. What really jammed my signal was that someone had slipped the t-square into my pocket, and I had no idea who or when. Why not just tell me face to face? Why all this secrecy? If they were so concerned, wouldn't they want to help me instead of making me play some kind of guessing game? I mean, I hadn't gotten on a murder-mystery cruise line.

The *Starshine* did offer basic security. I'd seen a couple of souped-up guards when I punched my voucher. I figured talking to one of them might be a logical first step. Maybe. If the amenities of the ship were any indication,

I highly doubted Desmo Voro Starshine sprang for top-notch security. They were more likely jump fighters looking to score some credits before landing their next ring gig.

Then there was the whole last-name issue. Thanks, Pops. No, what I needed to do was figure out who had the slippery fingers, corner them, and demand some answers. A kid picked up some stuff when they were dragged off to the worlds Pops picked to do his research on. Even further, a teenager on the verge of adulthood learned certain life lessons when their family name became a curse word. I wasn't too worried at the moment.

I put the t-square back in its case and tucked it between the bunk and the wall. The hiding spot wasn't the greatest, but my options were limited.

Time to mingle.

4

The Rat's out of the Dumpster

The final resting place of the *Rapscallion*, once the crown jewel in humanity's military fleet, was the muck and mud of Quarter's Landing, a dismal little planet where Leif Thropson attempted to establish a mining colony. The whole enterprise went down as an utter failure, and in a drunken stupor, Leif made a bet with a shrewd Yumi and lost the whole planet.

Quarter's Landing was a day's trip from Starbase 9.2, and having spent the majority of the day tucked away, I enjoyed freedom from the effervescent Mrs. Gol, who, thank Jupiter, had retired to her luxury suite in need of rest. Could she have slipped the t-square into my pocket? Possible but doubtful. She wasn't light on her feet, and I'd been painfully aware of her presence since we met. Could I rule her out? Nope. Not yet. I figured it was always good to keep my options open.

As I left my more-than-cozy hab-unit, the flashy, scrolling announcement strip embedded in the ship's hallways said we would dock in a little under twenty minutes, enough time to scope out all the possible suspects—namely, every passenger on the *Starshine*.

As I rounded a corner toward the observation deck, a cacophony of snorts, laughs, and dry, hacking coughs greeted me. Oh, goody. The hatchlings had escaped their nested wheelie cart. Annoying little chompers. But I couldn't stop my own chuckle from betraying me as I spied two of them latched onto one of the Star Eaters' robes. The Star Eaters weren't too impressed as they spun around, trying to catch the hatchlings.

I spied a bench tucked back against the far wall, devoid of bothersome individuals, and plopped down. According to Mrs. Gol, the cruise was barely full. What I saw was what I got. Everyone had brushed past me at some point while waiting to board the *Starshine* after the scintillating excursion onto Starbase 9.2. Any one of my fellow travelers could've slipped the t-square into my pocket, not to mention the brush with Mr. Soft-as-Thunder Voice in the hab-unit hallway.

I weighed the possibilities, ranking my fellow passengers according to ease of access to my person, which forced me to return to the most likely culprit, Mrs. Gol. The woman was the only one I'd had prolonged contact with. And she'd reached out to me in the first place. Had all her chattiness been a cover to try to make some kind of contact? What was up with her seeking me out to go on the tours with her? Loneliness or something else? Was it all a cover for something?

"Attention, honored guests. We will begin loading the shuttles momentarily."

The unwelcome intrusion upon my brooding forced me to stand and stretch. I tuned out the rest of the standard announcement and waited for everyone else to shuffle out.

Mr. Soft-as-Thunder Voice hadn't escaped my attention, slipping into the room shortly after me and standing off in one corner, his attention fixed on the Glipglow hatchlings' comedy hour. I noted Mr. Soft-as-Thunder stalled as well, nodding and gesturing for the others to go on ahead. Polite or intentional?

"There you are, dear."

Blasted things not very polite to repeat… The woman had found me.

"I can't wait to tour the *Rapscallion*," Mrs. Gol gushed.

I smiled my best nonthreatening smile and walked toward her, knowing that ignoring her wouldn't work. Mr. Soft-as-Thunder Voice nodded to both of us, earning a sniff and a scowl from Mrs. Gol and an inquisitive glance from me.

"You'll love it," the woman said. "To walk along the halls of a ship so talked about, so discussed throughout the stars… Oh, the notion gives me goose bumps."

I'm sure it does, I thought. As we moved out into the hallways, I couldn't help but blurt out, "Do you think there's any danger?"

So my tact and timing weren't great. But come on, if someone had slipped you a cryptic message warning about danger, wouldn't you want to figure it out?

Mrs. Gol's demeanor shifted noticeably, earning the rare occurrence of my full attention. The woman's entire body came to a dead stop then turned. The wrinkles around her eyes and lips deepened, and she had to lean back slightly to look me in the eyes. "Danger? Now, why would you ask such a question?"

I'll admit she kind of creeped me out a bit right there. Involuntarily, I took a step back as she reached out to try to pat my arm.

"Don't you worry. Your secret is safe with me."

"Excuse me?"

Mrs. Gol leaned closer. "I know who you are. What your father did. You don't think I would gallivant around with someone without running a background check, do you?"

That definitely wasn't what I'd been expecting.

"I don't know why your father did such a…" she paused, searching for some inoffensive term, "unexpected maneuver, but I can tell you're nothing like him, are you?"

I tried to smile, to regain my composure, but I suddenly felt as if I was the one on display rather than what the cruise had to offer.

"Come now. We need to catch up, or else we'll miss the tour."

That was that. Mrs. Gol turned and hobbled as fast as she could toward the transfer hub. I watched her go, a cascade of unwanted emotions and memories rooting me to the spot. If she was a purist, she wouldn't want to be seen with me. But then again, out there, who would see us together?

Her time spent with me would be a solid piece of gossip to take home. I imagined the stories. *"Oh, did I tell you about the time I shared a cruise with the most notorious human's daughter? I feared for my life the whole time. Who knows what type of bad egg she might be?"*

Mrs. Gol would take command of the center of attention, surrounded by other little old ladies gathered around platinum-inlaid tables and sipping on expensive teas and feigning admiration for their brave compatriot, who'd dared to be around someone like me. Children and grandchildren would admonish their matriarch for having taken such a risk, but they would always clamor for her to tell them the story just one more time in their best whiny voices.

"Excuse us."

I turned and raised an eyebrow at a human family behind me. The man scowled, while his two bored-looking kids threw me a wicked smile. I'd forgotten about them. When I didn't move fast enough for their liking, the two kids took off, knocking me out of the way. With no apologies, the man and woman followed after their errant offspring.

"Rude" was a mild way of putting it. But whatever, people.

If frustration wrapped in beautifully laminated layers of anxiety was on the menu, I'd been served up three giant helpings. Going back to the tiny, cramped hab-unit would only drive me nuts. Staying on the ship didn't appeal to me either. In fact, I tasted more than a teaspoon of anger, just to keep the whole food metaphor going—for fun, you know.

I felt as if those frustration-wrapped pastries had been filled with hundreds of juicy anger fruit. Each bite was bursting with spice, inflaming my tongue and body with enough anger to make me want to go see those fancy holographic sims Mrs. Gol prattled on about then cram a mouthful of repentance pie down her throat.

Okay, that last metaphor wasn't great.

Pops might've gone down the wrong history slide, but he'd been a good man. Have I gone looking for answers? You bet your shiny rocket, I have. Found any? Nope. But even though I don't know why he flipped and aided the Eeri during the war, I knew he had to have had a damn good reason to do so.

I gritted my teeth and prepared to do battle.

I made it all of two steps before my face went slack, my brain went, "What the…?" and I crumpled to the floor.

5

Unexpected Allies

The words "Wake up" preceded a sharp slap to my face.

My eyes flew open and landed on the fuzzy face of Mr. Soft-as-Thunder Voice.

"Get up and get moving."

Yeah, no. I tried—I honestly did. But I couldn't move my legs. I believe I tried to say as much, but based on his annoyance, the words from my brain didn't take the correct exit at my mouth.

I blinked and tried to focus as the man fumbled in his pockets for something. A fair amount of fear was coursing through me at that moment. That cryptic note about danger. Mrs. Gol admitted she knew about Pops. A sudden collapse. Now, this stranger, admittedly a very handsome stranger, was kneeling before me.

A rough-and tumble-voice filled the hallway. "Move away from her, you ghoul!"

Though relieved to discover I could turn my head, I wasn't so relieved to see one of the Glipglow parental figures doing the yelling.

You ever spent time at the Lunar History Zoo? Been

to the alligator or crocodile displays? Glipglows share an amazing similarity to those guys, only they've got a shorter snout and a lower jaw that splits in half, each complete with its own set of teeth. I don't envy them that dentist bill. They also have four upper-body appendages, with two legs for bipedal movement and a thick tail for added balance.

Watching one of those rushing toward me as my rescuer wasn't particularly comforting.

Mr. Soft-as-Thunder Voice jumped to his feet and flipped back the edge of his jacket. "Stop, I—"

No way was he going to be able to finish that sentence, as the entire corridor began to vibrate.

Interesting fact: Glipglows sport an impressive set of vocal tracts and an even more astonishing pair of lungs. A few reports have detailed those deep, resonant sounds, but on the whole, the species prefers privacy over the whole matter.

The vibration came in a series of long and short waves, which must've meant "Charge!" because all of a sudden, tiny miniatures of the adult rushed past the Glipglow and swarmed the man.

The situation would've been hilarious if not for my current state of fear. The man jumped up and down, swatting at the little guys and letting loose a series of "Ouch" and "Quit that" then a rather unpleasant "Yulp" as one of the Glipglow offspring chomped on his tail.

Another Glipglow adult appeared out of nowhere, moved to my side, and ran a cold talon down my cheek. Talk about invasion of privacy. I know what those nefarious talons are capable of. Glipglows have culti-vated an appearance of having an awkward relationship with technology when, in fact, they design a lot of cutting-edge tech coming down the chute. Those three-inch talons aren't just for defense. Everyone knows they're embedded with a whole spectrum of tech gadgets. Digital lockpicks, credit transfers, hacking software—you name it, and it was probably embedded in its coding.

"No fretting. Checking biochemical status."

The chaos of the tiny chomper army settled down, and the first Glipglow to my rescue moved to stand between my still uncooperative body and Mr. Covered in Bites but Still Handsome.

A series of clicks, guttural vocalizations, and complicated hand gestures ensued between the Glipglows. My eyes darted back and forth, but no matter how hard I concentrated, I didn't have a clue as to what was going to happen, only a sneaking suspicion if this incident had occurred on their home world, a particularly tall and delicious-looking specimen might find themselves on a roasting spit.

"Get off me," Mr. Not So Happy growled.

"We will report you," growled the Glipglow that wasn't getting up close and personal with me.

The one who'd checked my biostats stood, lower jaws opening and snapping shut. I wished they would move a few steps to the right. They were dripping saliva all over my legs.

"To whom?" The previously alluring violet in the man's irises darkened and turned a brilliant shade of emerald.

Bioupgrade? Cosmetic vanity? Unknown biological trait? So many questions. And don't forget that tail.

"To the captain. Do you not know who you're standing against?" my first Glipglow rescuer snapped.

The other Glipglow opened and closed its lower jaws while its body vibrated. Its companion turned, and another series of animated hand gestures ensued.

I wanted to know who Mr. Not So Happy was standing against, but he didn't seem to have gotten the memo, and he stepped forward. With a defiant flourish, he finished the gesture of pushing back his immaculately tailored jacket and produced a badge.

Unexpected. And unwanted.

If my brain could've coordinated with my mouth, it would've spewed a few choice words. Instead, I gave him the best glare I could manage. I worked hard to keep my nose clean, never wanting to interact with a badge again after my less-than-stellar experiences.

Apparently, the Glipglows and their offspring were also not impressed, as they all stood their ground. Good for them.

Stalemate it was, then.

"I'm a licensed agent of the InterGalactic Justice system."

"Not if they can't find you, you aren't," the larger of the two Glipglows growled.

I danced a little inside. Not that I wanted them to eat the handsome man, but at least I understood the basic intent of what the Glipglow adults had discussed. Go me.

"This woman is in danger. I've been assigned to protect her."

My eyebrows shot up at that. Good grief. I should have tumbled to the idea right away, when we'd been in the hallway together after Starbase 9.2. The tight space and accidental brush-up were a perfect setup for planting the t-square. And being all cryptic and not coming out and telling me anything was a typical IGJ response.

"This human's been poisoned. Class A, Subset 29J on the poison control index. If it doesn't receive medical attention within the next three minutes and forty-three seconds, it will expire," the Glipglow stated with confidence.

Um, what? I mean, I guess that made sense, considering how my body was refusing to cooperate. But poison? So last decade. Trendy assassins carried out their jobs with focused pinpoint laser technology. One pull of a trigger—or push of a button, depending on one's appendage situation—and the target would be down. No messy situations with waiting around or not calculating the correct dosage—just point and shoot.

Why are you looking at me like that? So I happen to like true-crime dramas.

"Antidote?" Mr. IGJ asked.

The Glipglows rattled off a series of chemical formulas, earning only a snarl from Mr. IGJ.

"Less tech and more practical. Will the ship's medical storage have it?"

The Glipglows conferred between themselves for a few tense moments then said, "Yes."

"Then come with me."

Mr. IGJ shook off the remaining hatchlings and scooped me up. The gesture might have made for a romantic rescue scene, minus the fact I was dead weight with drool running down my chin. The poison was moving past paralysis and rapidly toward shutting down my bodily functions.

I don't remember much after that, only flashes of an increasingly concerned Mr. IGJ watching over me. Maybe a scream or two as the hatchlings made sure the medical techs scrambled out of the way.

What I do remember is waking up in my hab-unit. But I found the room jam-packed with all my would-be rescuers. Mr. IGJ was sitting at the foot of my bunk, while the two adult Glipglows had joined hands, forming an impromptu jungle gym for their little ones to play on.

"What's… what's going on?" Speaking hurt, and I struggled to sit up.

Mr. IGJ stood and pushed me back down. "Don't try to speak, and don't move. Your body needs time to recover."

No one was going to tell me what to do. I struggled against his rather impressive strength before deciding it was better to rest.

But I did croak out another word: "Answers."

One of the Glipglows turned toward me. "We were successful in counteracting the poison."

Good thing I couldn't say much in response. I'd felt that was a no-brainer. Judging by the look on Mr. IGJ's face, he wasn't going to elaborate either. So we stayed there, packed like sardines in my tiny room, in silence. Well, relative silence. The hatchlings had a grand old time. I saw why Glipglow parental skin was thick and scaly.

Thankfully, I dozed off at some point, and when I woke, the Glipglows had left and Mr. IGJ had hauled in a chair and was scanning a torrent of info on the Sur-T Screen.

I tried to pretend to sleep for a while, wanting to see what held his interest, but I wasn't fooling anyone. Mr. IGJ closed out his work and turned to face me.

Why, oh why, was being poisoned how I'd ended up alone with a handsome man?

"What do you know about Jorge?"

"What?" My strength returning, I pushed myself up into a sitting position. I was also relieved to discover I was still in my jumpsuit.

"Jorge Silone-Ruger."

His laser-focused insistence annoyed me. He displayed no concern for how I was feeling, no *"How are you doing after being poisoned and experiencing a near-death situation?"*

I had been personally attacked by someone aboard the *Starshine*. Just flashing a fancy badge didn't mean he was connected with the InterGalactic Justice system. Those things could easily be replicated and passed off to a con artist.

A disturbing thought crossed my mind. What if he'd poisoned me and been caught in the act by the Glipglows? And where were they, anyway?

"No. I didn't poison you, and the Glipglows needed to break their fast. Turns out the first meal of the day is a family affair that can't be missed."

Um. Not cool, IGJ man.

"Telepath?" I asked.

A spark of emerald appeared in his violet eyes. "Only when I'm stressed and the subject is uncooperative."

"Uncooperative? I've just been poisoned, and you're acting like I'm the criminal."

I'll admit a flash of fear tore through me as he leaped up and growled. Yes. Full-on growled. "You may not be complicit, but you've got to know something. Tell me about Jorge."

Okay, enough was enough, fear or no fear. I might not have leaped to my feet, but I got up off my bunk, stumbled over to him, and poked him in the chest. "I've done nothing wrong but be the object of someone's nefarious schemes. You've got no right to treat me this way. If you don't back off, I'll contact my lawyers at Bloodhearst & Strobe."

I hear you. I know I've been complaining about not having enough credits for all those shiny baubles. Confore doesn't pay much, that's for damned sure. I barely scratch by with my weekly allotment of credits. But I won't hide the fact Pops left a tidy sum of money behind. I've simply learned not to touch it, leaving the credits for emergency purposes only.

Such as this.

Being interrogated for nearly a year had been exhausting, both mentally and physically. As soon as Pops's accounts had cleared, a small miracle in and of itself, I'd hired the best attorneys.

"The state of innocence has yet to be determined," Mr. IGJ muttered.

I'd hoped my determined posturing would spark a small measure of respect. It might have if I hadn't collapsed, left to glare at him from an undignified position at his feet.

Pretending my collapse was in fact planned, I asked, "Why were you assigned to protect me, then? If you don't believe I'm innocent, shouldn't you have arrested me? Or even walked away after I had been poisoned?"

Mr. IGJ's tail whipped back and forth, snagged the corner of the chair, and pulled the seat forward. So, not cosmetic vanity but a prehensile tail. Interesting.

Even though purist ideology still existed, several underground enclaves of cosmetic surgeons would do anything for the right amount of credits. Not that I would have pegged Mr. IGJ for that sort of individual, but one never knows. I wasn't up to date on the latest with Darquet physiology or the outcomes of introducing another species's DNA. Perhaps Mr. IGJ's tail was natural after all.

I couldn't help but dig at the man a little more. "I mean, let's face it. The IGJ isn't known for its stellar work or integrity. Not unless you've got credits to last you two or three lifetimes."

The tail twitched again, and emerald crept into the edges of his irises. "Despite popular misgivings, the IGJ values its code of ethics, inclusivity amongst a wide variety of species, and mission to uphold justice amongst the participating worlds."

"Nice company speech. Now, tell me how you really feel."

Mr. IGJ got back to his feet, and I could literally feel the anger radiating off the man, I kid you not. Definitely a telepath, and a dangerous one if he couldn't keep his emotions under control. Rumors about the ancient Darquets abounded, as well as even more salacious gossip concerning what mixing bloodlines produced.

I would be lying if I said meeting a man of mixed Darquet ancestry didn't spike my curiosity a little. But that wasn't the time. Someone had tried to kill me. I would be dammed before I would let them get off this godforsaken cruise ship before I'd figured out why.

The aftereffects of either the poison or its antidote had left the ache of tight muscles, too long cramped. I winced as I worked to rearrange myself into a somewhat more dignified position leaning against the wall.

"So you're assigned to me, huh?"

Mr. IGJ refused to look at me. Instead, he focused on the blank screen. "Yes."

Mysterious men of few words frequented my dreams, but that experience was taking a decidedly different turn.

"An explanation would be appreciated."

"My supervising commander flashed this assignment. I happened to be the one to pick it up."

"That's not very comforting."

"It's not meant to be."

That stung, I admit. My history with the IGJ—or any other governing authority—wasn't great, but they take an oath or something. But I hadn't flashed some crank calls or tried to get into the news-junkie wannabe crowd to warrant this IGJ visit. Someone was legitimately out for my blood. I pay taxes and social welfare add-ons and haven't been tagged since my father's death. I was afforded some measure of courtesy.

"I'm owed answers." I used the best no-nonsense

customer-service voice I could muster, the one saved for those oh-so-special callers who just happen to be experts in tech and needed someone to help, and I air quote here, "confirm" their "suspicions."

Praise the gods of all that's holy, my line worked. Mr. IGJ snapped to attention and looked right at me.

"Then talk to me about Jorge Silone-Ruger."

Saturn's rings. It didn't work. I shrugged. Two could play that game.

"Why?" I asked.

"Any information you can share regarding the whereabouts of Jorge would be helpful for the IGJ."

Before I could muster a witty comeback, the Sur-T Screen lit up, accompanied by an annoying alarm. The phrase Urgent Message scrolled across the screen, along with a notification of how long the message had been buffered in the system.

Mr. IGJ leaned forward to snooze the alert.

"Hold on, Mr. Cryptic," I said. "I want to know what the message is."

"It's not important."

"They don't label them urgent for the fun of it," I snapped. "Play the message."

He wasn't happy, but he did.

Mrs. Gol's voice blared through my room. "I just heard! Are you all right, dear? Do you need anything? I can talk with the captain and get you clearance for assistance bots. You really shouldn't miss out on the chance to tour the *Rapscallion*. There's still plenty of time to come down and join me."

"Are you kidding me?"

Whoops. Did I say that out loud? I shouldn't have been surprised that the nosy woman had ferreted out why I wasn't by her side, eagerly waiting to see the nuclear meltdown of what promised to be a horrendous obscuring of historical accuracy.

"It's not a bad idea."

My eyes whipped up to Mr. IGJ. "What?"

"The Glipglows are quite knowledgeable. You should have regained rudimentary mobility by now."

I'm not a fool. I knew what he was insinuating. He was going to use me as bait.

"Under a few conditions."

6

The Skinny
(and I Do Mean Skinny)
on Project Clear Sight

As Mr. IGJ searched my carefully crafted deadpan expression, a slight narrowing of his eyes produced a small furrow of uncertainty between his brows. Call me whatever you want, but that little wrinkle just about ironed out my resolve. Don't ask me why. Perhaps it deepened his chiseled features or appeared to signal his concern over my situation. I didn't know.

"I want answers. Why do you care so much about Jorge? Why am I being targeted? And don't wait next time. I would prefer not to have a near-death experience again."

I swear the man snorted at me.

"First, we'll be lucky if the assassin tries again during the cruise unless the Glipglows haven't blown my cover. I doubt the suspect is going to just point and shoot, not in a heavily monitored tourist ship, even if it is a little light on the tourists."

"Lucky?"

His eyes shone a deep crimson, vibrating with intensity. "But wandering around at a tourist stop, where any number of accidents could befall an eager tourist, would be worth another try. They've missed their chance, and now, either they're going to be desperate to try again or another contract will be opened."

I paused my efforts to stand, and I glared at the man. "Another contract?"

If someone or something had gone to the trouble negotiating a contract for my death, the situation was far more serious than I'd realized. I twisted and, with a clumsy hop, collapsed on my bunk.

"The IGJ regularly monitors contract channels."

That meant I rated higher than I would've thought, if the IGJ had seen my name and flagged the contract for investigation.

"Look, I don't know Jorge. I've never even met the man. He works in a different department. I've only seen his name on the employee rosters. And if this has anything to do with my pops, then you should know I have no idea what he got mixed up in. He didn't involve me."

He tilted his head to one side. "It's not believed this is connected to your father."

My stomach soured. "Then what in Pluto's dilemma is going on?"

"That's what I'm here to find out."

"Besides making sure I stay alive, right?" I said, half

in jest. "Right?" I drew out the word with as much force as I could muster.

His tail twitched before he gave me the decency of at least a curt nod. "The IGJ would prefer you live through this, yes."

Good thing the guy hadn't gone into the medical field. His bedside manner definitely left something to be desired.

That strength I had hoped to replenish was gone. My entire body felt sluggish, as though I'd entered one of those infamous orbital-station races. Why anyone would want to run through increasing levels of gravity until they were bleeding out of the ears, eyes, and nose is anyone's guess. And get this. It's usually the rock hoppers that race. You won't find cloud jumpers or spacers doing such crazy stunts.

"You still haven't answered any of my questions."

Expertly ignoring me once again, he moved with one solid stride to the door and tapped at the comm panel.

"Starshine Directory. How may we help you today?"

"I need a word with the captain," Mr. IGJ stated.

"I'm sorry, the captain is currently unavailable. Perhaps one of our—"

"This is Turen ed-Suren with the InterGalactic Justice system. Confirmation bio-ID alpha, seven, twenty-four, tango, thirty-three."

After a squeal of concern on the other end, a gruff voice came over the comm system. "Yeah, so? What do you want?"

Was I expecting something else, like the polite or

cultured response of a captain who'd undergone years of flight school, AI integration surgeries, and psychology? Nope. My expectations had left the bay long before. More than likely, the captain was from a line of long-haul smugglers and knew all the tricks of keeping a ship together within a shoestring budget.

Turen didn't miss a beat. "I'm requesting the use of two assistance bots for use on the *Rapscallion* tour." He paused and added, "Bill it to my central account and feel free to do a commission add-on for your stellar service, Captain."

That was unexpected. At least I had a name for Mr. IGJ Man.

He turned and raised an eyebrow. "I'm not a fresh cloud hopper. And I prefer Cain." He must've realized he'd done it again, as he whipped around, waiting for the Captain's response.

<Stay out of my head,> I growled inwardly for good measure and watched his tail whip back and forth in pleasure.

"Two assistance bots are being programmed and will head to your current location. Is there anything else I can help you with?" the captain asked.

"No, thank you. Not at this moment."

As he turned to face me, I scowled and crossed my arms for good measure, just in case he couldn't pick up on my current torrent of thoughts.

"Fine," he snapped. That delicious spark of emerald appeared in his eyes before he regained control. "When one of the IGJ's operatives went missing, a general inquiry case appeared on the books."

Finally. Answers. "But what does that have to do with Jorge? Or me?"

"That agent was embedded at Confore, and the general inquiry has been upgraded to a murder investigation."

I felt as if I'd been poisoned all over again. Bile stung my throat, and I couldn't stop my gag reflex. I knew I should've eaten off the buffet and been done with the whole cursed cruise.

The mattress shifted under Turen—no, sorry, Cain's additional weight. There was a story about his name, which needed ferreting out at some point.

"Here." Against the smooth skin of his palm lay a small green pill and a slightly larger yellow one. "One will help with the muscle cramps. The other's for energy."

I eyed the peace offering but shook my head. I did appreciate the abrupt turnabout of compassion, but pills were something I avoided, especially stims. Let's just say I'd had a bad experience with them and leave it at that.

His hand closed around the two pills and tucked them back into a pocket. "How long have you worked for Confore Tech?" The question was unexpected.

"Shouldn't that be in my file?" I put more venom in those words than I meant. Whatever momentary truce had started, died.

Cain stood. "It was. Answer the question."

"Five years. Roughly."

"And before that?"

"Whimsical Heights," I muttered. That was one of the many companies the Weplies had bought out.

"How long?"

"Look, if you're not going to help me, then just float off. I haven't done anything wrong."

"How long?"

If I had been up to full power, I would've stormed out, paced up and down the halls, and told this piece of space junk how I truly felt. Then I would've contacted my lawyers and gotten his badge revoked.

But I didn't have to. I broadcasted my feelings quite well.

Emerald bled into violet, and he growled at me, a full-on growl with enough lip action to reveal two very sharp canines. "They said you'd be uncooperative. No wonder no one wanted your case."

I was surprised and not surprised. My time with the IGJ after everything with Pops wasn't a Scouts of the Universe networking conference. But hearing those words out loud still stung.

"Then why don't you just leave? I'll figure it out. It's not like this is the first time I've been abandoned." Whoops—I hadn't meant to say that, but in hindsight, my admission was exactly what needed to be said.

After a long pause, Cain exhaled and took a seat. "Project Clear Sight is what the IGJ administration has dubbed their case against Confore Tech. It began as an inquiry into smuggling and trading outside sanctioned corporations. Hints and whispers only. But enough for the IGJ to authorize inside surveillance."

To say I felt shocked at his candor would've been an understatement. My wounded pride whispered unkind words to throw at the man, but I'd learned once someone started talking, keeping them going was best.

"Jorge."

He nodded. "Everything seemed fine. Regular reports, no disturbance within Wepli security protocols. Then the reports stopped. Jorge was gone. First thing the IGJ's internal department does is look for a turnaround, an agent paid off or now dealing for the other side. But there wasn't anything that rated further investigation on that front, only a missing agent and an extremely friendly Wepli contact.

"When Jorge's body turned up on Lunar 5, a full investigation had been authorized. No foul play was discovered, but no real, solid conclusion was formed as to why Jorge had been on Lunar 5 or why he'd gone silent. The IGJ closed the case and buried Project Clear Sight."

Great. That didn't sound good. The IGJ did a decent job at keeping the peace. For the most part. The organization worked at keeping the peace between the myriad of species interconnected through trade routes and relationships. But the IGJ only went so far, which wasn't a secret when it came to governmental affairs or corporations. The fact they'd even started a case against Confore Tech was a small miracle in and of itself.

"What does this have to do with me? I work for the help desk."

"I don't know." He shifted his weight and tilted his head, studying me and making me blush under his scrutiny. "All I know is the IGJ caught the contract on your head and sent out the assignment."

"So you just assumed I knew something about what happened to Jorge and this whole Project Clear Sight deal?"

"It was a logical leap. Only two humans have ever worked for Weplies, Jorge and yourself. Jorge's dead. And now someone wants you dead as well. Either there's a connection between the fact you both are of the same species, or you've got a connection to the original investigation the IGJ doesn't know or isn't willing to share."

"Or," I added, "the Weplies figured out what the IGJ was up to. And made an assumption I was a spy like Jorge."

"Which would explain this cruise trip."

I hadn't considered that. Goose bumps covered my arms as the door's chime sounded. His hand flew to his right hip as his posture shifted. Nonmilitary ships maintained a standard no-weapon policy—too many hotheads out there with lousy aim. Especially on older ships, like this one, screens and fancy decorations hid the sensitive equipment required to maintain our bubble of safety in the vast death trap of space.

The door slid open, and one of the ship's staff threw Cain a sour look as he handed over the bots. With more than a few mumbled curse words, some blushes, and another growl, he got the bots strapped to my legs and lower back.

The units were stiff and, even after a few calibration attempts, refused to move in sync with my body. "How am I supposed to duck for cover in these monstrosities?"

"Just pray you won't have to."

"Oh, how comforting."

I moved back and forth a few times in the cramped quarters, not thrilled about his plan. Stopping in front of him, I couldn't resist poking him in the chest, purely for the purpose of enunciating my words. "Let's get this straight. I don't know anything about what happened to Jorge. Or any smuggling or illicit trading. I do my job. And I keep my nose clean." I took a step back. "You're the telepath, right? Then you should know I'm telling the truth."

His upper lip quivered. "All I can tell is you believe you're telling me the truth."

I drew in a deep breath, but he wouldn't give me the satisfaction.

"But," he said, sounding reluctant, "I believe you. I'll do my job of protecting you. But I can't do that if I don't know who the hired assassin is."

Crickets all around.

Not only did I want to know who'd put out the contract on me and why, I needed to know more about that stupid Project Clear Sight and what'd happened to Jorge. At times, I wished Pops hadn't encouraged my curiosity.

7

A Planet of Puke
(Kind of—You'll See)

Before we left, I pinged Mrs. Gol to assure her that I was up for coming on the tour and would find her at the Quarter's Landing's shuttle pads. Cain turned out to be great at spending credits, and after a few generous tips, the shuttle crew took us down, giddy over their newfound wealth.

The transport from the ship to land lasted a little over half an hour, more than enough time to sort through the information Cain had given up. Smuggling wasn't a big deal. All the major corporations engaged in the practice, keeping multiple sets of books. Governments changed the rules on trading restrictions so frequently that the black market sported the only reliable source for and stable quantities of goods on the market since no one in the black-market line of work gave a hoot about red tape.

Trading, on the other hand, was different. The Jumjul regulated the trade of stocks and credits. They were a no-nonsense species whose religion centered around mathematics and the various branches of studies related to numbers—not to mention their military genius.

The history books talk about a grand and glorious sit-down between the Jumjuls, corporate CEOs, and the Old Earth Monarchy. Teachers led discussions and historical recreations of the event, with students clamoring to portray the mighty Jumjul. Pops spent some time on New Earth 3.0 and enrolled my brother and me in a standard school.

Biggest mistake ever.

Pops exposed us to a lot more than what was typically taught in schools, and our teachers quickly grew tired of our corrections to the history books. By the time the school play rolled around, featuring—you guessed it—the Jumjul Delegation of the Cosway, my brother and I had been expelled.

The truth is that the history books glossed over the bloody conflicts leading up to the negotiations. No one wanted to remember the skirmishes or how the Jumjuls' military had simply been superior. Throw in a dash of fear over angering the Jumjul again, and it was a recipe for eliminating the unsavory bits of history. And even though military might and tech had moved forward for several species, including humans, no one could match the Jumjul. The fear that species inflicted made them the perfect suit-and-tie-wearing, briefcase-toting group to oversee trades.

If the IGJ suspected the Weplies of illicit trading, the suspicion should've been passed on to the Jumjul. Or at the least, they should've handed the case over once it started. That the IGJ hadn't handed the case over meant either the IGJ was beginning to challenge Jumjul authority, which didn't bode well for anyone, or the suspicion of illicit trading was a cover-up for something else. That wouldn't be good either because if trade concerns were being used as a cover, then whatever this case of the IGJ's was covering up was far worse than angering the Jumjul. That was something I couldn't wrap my head around.

I wondered if Cain had figured this out. I couldn't be sure—too many unanswered questions. Why had he picked up my case when no one else wanted it? Looking for promotion? Just too stupid to realize what he was doing? Or perhaps too desperate?

He didn't strike me as desperate or dumb. He obviously wasn't letting go of that Project Clear Sight deal. So what wasn't he telling me?

"Prepare for landing." The shuttle's notification wasn't as courteous as the ship's announcements, but at least it was enough warning to buckle up.

I didn't care what rating the pilot might be sporting. Landings always held risk, and thanks to ChowHo Insurance, shuttles came equipped with Confore's Crash 'n' Ride safety harnesses. Any impact would activate the harnesses, triggering expansion into a trade-secret material designed to protect passengers from crashing or flying debris. All those ancient movies and television shows when humanity imagined living amongst the stars were chock-full of character injuries due to the lack of seat belts. Go figure.

I clipped my harness together, and unease settled

over me. Whatever Project Clear Sight was really about, it'd laid the seeds of doubt about the Weplies and Confore. Their tech was everywhere and in pretty much everything. Humanity and several other species relied heavily on what Confore Tech produced. If something nefarious was afoot, would every piece of tech come under suspicion?

Truth be told, I would much prefer dealing with an endless life of Help Desk calls, sorting out that mess, to seeing the *Rapscallion* and Mrs. Gol and risking another go-around with my potential assassin. And while I'm being honest, Cain's presence wasn't a huge comfort at that point either.

Landing went off without a hitch. At least Desmo Voro Starshine Adventures sprang for decent shuttle pilots. I would give them a star for that.

When I exited the shuttle, Mrs. Gol, true to form, was waiting for me. Seeing my escort earned her a narrowing of my eyes and a suspicious frown, but the assistance bots were diverting her attention, thankfully.

"I received the alert you were shuttling down. No one would tell me what happened, only that an injury had occurred and medical treated it," she lamented.

"Turns out the vending machine isn't any better than the buffet." I surprised myself with how smoothly the lie rolled off my tongue.

"There was a glitch with the system, and Ms. Mahia ended up with neurotoxin poisoning," Cain said.

I couldn't help but shoot a look of incredulity at his smooth follow-up lie. That didn't exactly score him points in the trustworthiness department. Judging by the look he returned, he was thinking the same. Fine. At least we were even.

Mrs. Gol, ignoring Cain, clucked her tongue and shook her head. "Poor thing. What a horrible way to spend the rest of your vacation. And especially here, at the best part. We'll just have to make do."

We? I couldn't help but be a little affronted. I was the one who'd been poisoned and dragged down there according to someone else's plan, which was seeming like an increasingly bad idea as I tried to follow—"tried" being the operative word.

Cain, to his credit, didn't push against the fact that Mrs. Gol ignored him, yet I could see irritation in his stiff shoulders and clenched jaw. To my disappointment, I sympathized with the IGJ man. I kept my surname quiet for the same reason, and while I generally ignored the frowns, scowls, and outright slurs when people realized who my pops was, I'd never actually gotten used to it.

"The holographic displays they've added really bring this whole part of the tour to another level," Mrs. Gol claimed.

"How quaint," I muttered.

"I have never had the opportunity to tour this particular piece of history," Cain interjected politely.

Mrs. Gol paused her diatribe then, addressing me instead of Cain, launched into her tour guide persona. I mostly ignored her regurgitated pamphlet information and considered what I knew of the unappealing little planet.

The whole mining dream had been a joke. Quarter's Landing was nothing but a swampy, foul-smelling ball of puke. Yup, you heard me. Puke—that revolting color of greasy slime flecked with chunks of chewed-up food. Picture that, and you've got Quarter's Landing down pat. The Yumi who'd won the planet hadn't minded, building a refueling station and doing a fair amount of business. Despite its less-than-appealing environment and aesthetic, Quarter's Landing was in the perfect location for freighters to refuel or dump waste when trading between Glipglow space and Torth's Portals.

Whoever financially backed the tours of the *Rapscallion* had gone to considerable length to beautify the shuttle landing pads and the concourse to the infamous ship. We suffered through a few minutes of odoriferous swamp perfume before entering a brightly lit walkway walled in with smart glass. The images changed as we walked toward the tour's entrance. Peppered throughout the ads were rotating pictures of the *Rapscallion's* construction, the ceremony for its maiden voyage, and commissioned works of the ship at its finest during battle.

The concourse narrowed considerably, forcing the crowds to move single file through the last of the entrance. The images switched from advertising the *Rapscallion's* history to the plethora of vendors a tourist could spend their hard-earned credits on. I will give Mrs. Gol some credit. If the adverts were even partly true in their representations of all the collectibles, some halfway decent items were available.

One piece that caught my eye was touted to be from the Arts Enclaves on Yyu. The Arts Enclaves welcomed anyone of any species, provided they passed the entrance exams and could pay the hefty entrance fee. Truly talented individuals typically wound up with sponsors, despite the prevalence of nasty rumors about how the artists were treated more like personal property than the recipients of honest philanthropy.

A spun-crystal representation of the *Rapscallion* was labeled with only a number, meaning a lower-level artist had crafted it. Once enough of an artist's pieces sold, along with the artist passing several grueling tests in their respective art field, the artist's name would then be attached to their work. For collectors, one favorite pastime was to guess which older pieces might belong to a master's art, which they fought over in high-end auctions and black-market deals.

"Tickets, please." A bored-looking Neetho extended a tentacle.

"We're with the *Starshine*." Mrs. Gol sniffed.

"We're sorry. That tour has already been accounted for. Tickets, please."

"But there were extenuating circumstances. We're not paying for something which we've already paid for."

"That tour has been accounted for. Tickets, please."

Cain stepped between Mrs. Gol and the Neetho ticket taker. Mrs. Gol practically vibrated with affronted sensibilities. I smothered a laugh.

"How much for three tickets?"

A few more tentacles waved around. "Two hundred and thirty-nine credits."

"That's outrageous," Mrs. Gol said. "How dare you—"

Cain turned to face her, and the cramped quarters made it impossible for her to escape him. With her attention focused on Cain, I didn't restrain my maniacal grin of pleasure. Of course, it was immediately followed by a rush of guilt. Mrs. Gol had been rather kind to me even if I found her lectures dull and erroneous. Plus, Cain flashed me a rather nasty look. I'm not perfect, okay?

"I will be glad to help in this matter. Ms. Mahia has told me how much she was looking forward to seeing this part of the tour with you, Mrs. Gol. She said you are a kind and understanding woman. Please allow me to assist."

Okay, where were all those high-society manners before? He could've tried that approach rather than the whole uptight-and-annoying bit. I might've just melted into a puddle of goo and been a lot more cooperative.

Mrs. Gol's shoulders hunched forward, and she swung her head to try to peer at me. I put on my best fake honest smile. It must have worked because she returned the smile and nodded.

"That'll be fine," she said.

The Neetho accepted the credit transfer, handed Cain three tickets, and promptly waved another tentacle at him. "Tickets, please."

I rolled my eyes as Cain handed the tickets back.

"Welcome to the *Rapscallion*. Tour times are posted to your left as you enter. Feel free to come and go as you please, but if you exit, you will not be allowed to enter without a ticket. Vendors are located throughout the ship. Enjoy."

What a rousing and inspiring speech...

As we moved past the ticket booth, Mrs. Gol pushed past Cain and scuttled over to the tour board. "We're well past our original scheduled time, but no matter. We can go at our own pace."

Great. That translated to a snail's pace, as she would undoubtedly regale me with every excruciating piece of knowledge Mrs. Gol thought she knew about the ship. As I slid further into despair, her incessant need to read and reread displays would make for the perfect chance for the assassin to try again. We would be separated from the main group, therefore less likely to get help, and I was physically compromised, an easy target with an easier explanation for why I would be dead. Touring an old ghost ship without a tour guide surely created beautiful loopholes for ChowHo Insurance.

I edged closer to Cain. "You'd better be damned good at your job."

He shot me a look but refused to answer. That figured.

"What do you think?" Mrs. Gol asked. "Follow the map? Or go where we please?"

The question took me by surprise. I was sure Mrs. Gol would've been a stickler for following the map and whatever logical timeline the developers believed they'd laid down for their tourists.

"Let's follow the map," I answered. That would at least give me time to prepare mentally for whatever was coming.

With a satisfied expression, Mrs. Gol took the lead and launched into the history of the *Rapscallion*.

8

The Tour From...
Well, You Know

Constructed a few years before the advent of the Cricade Wars, the *Rapscallion* had boasted the best humanity's military offered: advanced weaponry, shielding, jump-drive cores, and the newly implemented cloaking technology. It was a beast of a ship yet deft at maneuvering. Maintained by over five hundred crew members and large enough to house roughly a thousand troops, the *Rapscallion* was armed with stealth fighters, roll-abouts, and hatchbacks. It had enjoyed a bloated career before the skirmishes fell into out-and-out war with the Eeri.

The news cycles followed the ship's battles with relish, detailing the lives of the brave crew and personnel. The scientists, engineers, and architects credited with bringing the *Rapscallion* to life were interviewed and offered coveted sponsorship positions with all the major advertising companies and were held up as heroes for humanity.

When the true force of the Eeri arrived, everything

fell apart. If any species maintained the resources and might to match the Jumjul, it was the Eeri. The breadth of their ship configurations and armaments was above par, which put the *Rapscallion* through the wringer.

Doubt spread as reports came in, concerning the damage the jewel of humanity had suffered. When the death tolls became public knowledge, anger flared through most of humanity's colonies. What was this ship doing? The miracle warship leading our fleet was supposed to keep us safe. Had all the publicity and news reports been a lie? Public sentiment began to change, and the news cycles ate it up, only spreading more vicious gossip and fear.

Nothing had been wrong with the *Rapscallion* or its crew, nor the hundreds of men and women trained to fight to the death to preserve our species. Humanity had been arrogant enough to think we'd finally built something tough enough to stand up to the majority of the "bad guys" out there in the universe, the Jumjul notwithstanding.

At the height of the war, the *Rapscallion* won the majority of battles it'd engaged in, but the news ran with only the losses, speculating on how leadership strategy had failed, who should take command after such embarrassing losses, and the like. Even though humanity and its allies had beaten back the Eeri, the damage had been done. The schematics for other similar ships were blackballed and a new class of warship developed.

Yet in the end, the *Rapscallion*, her crew, and all those she'd carried into battle had a glorious moment of redemption. They dealt the Eeri forces a devastating blow at Rackmore's Edge, and at first, surrender appeared to have been on the horizon.

But the vicious cloud-suckers saved the best for last. Or rather, they saved the unthinkable for a last resort. The Eeri turned the last of their warships into bombs. Three massive ships were sent to destroy their targets: Old Earth, Cloud-11, and Torth's Portals. All were places where humanity was the dominant species.

The coders aboard the *Rapscallion* figured out the Eeri's plans first. Captain Uriku Tow immediately issued orders to triage her ship's wounds and gave a rousing speech about being the last bastion of hope for humanity. She deployed what remained of the stealth fighters and roll-abouts. Each small fleet was successful in destroying the Eeri death ships before they reached their targets. Also, the fleets captured not only two of the highest-ranking Eeri commanders and a prominent religious leader for the Eeri but also the notorious Wats Hawking Orion.

My pops.

The one human known to have sided with the Eeri.

I think we can all agree on why I was less than thrilled to be doing this tour, potential assassination aside.

At the first stop on the map, the grand entrance to the *Rapscallion*, or rather the one transfer hub still located above the stink of the swamp, held a handful of food vendors. My stomach rumbled, and I realized I hadn't eaten anything since Starbase 9.2.

To Mrs. Gol's credit, she didn't mention my unbecoming stomach noises but simply suggested a light snack to take with us on the tour. This time, she insisted on paying. Cain declined her offer, which seemed to score him a few points.

I was pleased to see the owners weren't Jips but human, so at least the food should've been safe to eat. There's food, then there's food that has stood the test of time. No matter how humanity ages or where they travel amongst the stars, traditional dishes can be found at all human-owned food vendors. It's a time-honored tradition and a way to pay homage to our past.

My mouth watered at the two corn dogs handed over by the young woman behind the counter. I devoured the first one before Mrs. Gol received her order, and the second was gone before we set foot on the ship. I was still hungry. Sigh.

The interior walls of the *Rapscallion* gleamed in the vibrant lighting. The less-than-desirable remnants of battle had long since been cleaned and removed. A few strategic impact scars had been left for maximum tourist effect, but the visceral reminders of how devastating battle could be, even on board a well-armed ship, had vanished.

Crew pictures lined the walls of the transfer hub, beginning with command and working their way through the ranks. Beyond the photos were the names of the men and women who'd fought and lived on the *Rapscallion*. Each name was engraved on a brass plaque and displayed according to military ranking. More than a few names held asterisks at the end, indicating death in the line of service.

I didn't seek out my next thought, but it came nonetheless: what would all these people say, knowing that

I, the daughter of the infamous man who'd aided their greatest enemy, was about to walk through the ship they'd died and bled for?

A hand brushed against my arm, causing me to flinch, but the gesture also pushed the question aside. The hand wasn't Mrs. Gol's, who'd stopped behind me to admire the pictures, her head tilted up to stare misty-eyed at the command pictures.

"You have nothing to do with what happened," Cain stated quietly.

The words were unexpected, almost unwelcome. But not quite. I had to turn away and blink back tears. No one had said that to me before, not even the IGJ, who believed Pops had acted alone, leaving my brother and me to fend for ourselves while he went off and did God knows what. But no one had ever said as much. I had simply been released with a few gruff warnings then signed the papers when my case had been officially closed. My own lawyers never said a word about my innocence, always sidestepping anything that could come back to haunt them.

"The next stop is a communications node," Mrs. Gol declared without consulting the map clutched in her hand.

If I'd been touring any other ship—and I do mean any other ship, even a waste barge—the tech would have caught my interest. I just couldn't work up any enthusiasm as we traipsed behind Mrs. Gol, listening to her spout innocuous fact after fact. We passed several communication nodes, rec halls, training rooms, and the like. Annoyingly, Mrs. Gol stopped at every vendor we passed too. I'll admit I saw a few pieces that might have been worth some credits, but nothing was worthy enough to take home as a souvenir.

Oh, yes, do come into my humble abode. What's that, you ask? Why, that's a replica of the *Rapscallion*, the ship that captured and more than likely executed my pops. Makes a stunning centerpiece, doesn't it? Something to remind me of the absolute waste heap my life has become. Oh, yes. Thank you. The piece did set me back a few credits.

Right.

Winding our way through the decks, I became bored and increasingly agitated. I didn't want to be there. Nothing exciting was happening despite Cain perking up now and then at some uneventful noise. Watching Mrs. Gol shake her head, motion us forward, then say with a friendly conspiratorial look, "The best is yet to come," was growing tedious.

Sure. Okay. Whatever.

By the time we were a deck shy of command, I forgot all about any potential assassins. All I could think about was how I was walking where Pops had been. The majority of his arrest records were still sealed, and all I'd been able to glean was that he'd been captured, arrested, and detained on the *Rapscallion* for several months. Where he'd been moved after that, I had never been able to crack. For quite some time, I believed he was still alive, tucked away on a prison station or penal colony. But as the years passed, I knew the most realistic scenarios were either he'd died while being held on this ship, or he'd been transferred, interrogated, and executed.

My emotions didn't know what to do. I'd never wanted to go there. Maybe I'd always been afraid of learning something horrible, of realizing Pops didn't have some mysterious, profound reason to do what he did. But there I was, walking through the last known place he'd been alive.

My entire body felt numb, I grew lightheaded, and the corridor spun. Despite the clumsy support from the assistance bots, I shot out a hand to grab the wall but found something warm instead. Cain assisted me to a small alcove complete with a cushioned bench and pillows. My head flopped down between my legs, and I leaned into a hand rubbing circles across my back.

Imagine my shock when I realized Mrs. Gol was taking time out of her experience of the *Rapscallion* for the umpteenth time, rubbing my back. I gave her a weak but appreciative smile before my head dropped again, and I caught the flash of boots stalking back and forth in front of the alcove.

"I'm fine," I managed to croak. "Really. It's just a little overwhelming."

I had no need to hide. Both of them knew who I was and who my pops had been.

"Do you think you'll be able to finish, dear?"

Heat rose to my cheeks, and my hands curled into fists, but I managed to keep my voice even. "I think so."

Who cared? I mean, come on, folks.

For the first time, Mrs. Gol directly addressed Cain. "Be a sport and get some water, would you?"

Despite the lightheadedness, I looked at Mrs. Gol in shock then saw my expression mirrored on Cain's face.

"That would be helpful," I croaked.

He frowned.

"I'll be fine. We'll wait here."

<There's no one else around,> I thought. *<We'll stay here, and you'll be back in a flash. I'm no good to you like this. Get a splash of lemon with it, and I'll be good to resume my impression of bait dangling from a hook.>*

"Perhaps there will be a refreshment station up ahead," Cain countered.

The moment of civility passed.

Mrs. Gol stiffened as she replied sharply, "Then perhaps I will inform the captain how uneasy I feel in your presence. I'm sure he will understand how important it is to keep a woman of my substantial wealth satisfied with his management of the cruise."

After a rather long and intense stare, which would've been welcome at a very different time and setting, Cain gave me a tense nod and jogged off. No one needed to be a telepath to understand the turmoil he felt. Upsetting Mrs. Gol might force Cain to tip his hand as an IGJ agent. But more than that, her complaints would only lead to the uncomfortable and humiliating reality of dealing with such blatant prejudice.

Not that Mrs. Gol shouldn't be confronted over such matters, but that simply wasn't the time or the place. Too bad.

Maybe if I'd been in tip-top shape, I would've thought things through a little better. But the last vendor was only a deck below us, and I was confident I would be safe until Cain returned. I knew Cain wouldn't waste any time getting there and back.

"Is it difficult to confront the reality of your family's legacy?"

My head shot up, and I stared at Mrs. Gol. She continued to rub my back while her question dripped with poison.

"What's that supposed to mean?" Of course, I knew what she meant. I just felt flummoxed by the abrupt turnabout.

"Don't worry, dear. There'll be time enough to answer my question… and many more. All you need to do is sleep now."

I should've realized. She wasn't a sweet old lady, spoiled and rich, with credits to burn. I wasn't some curiosity she could talk up to her family and friends. I was her target.

"You. You poisoned me!"

She cocked her head to one side. "No, dear. I didn't have a hand in what happened before. Thank goodness at that too. Or else my plans would've been spoiled. And yes, I knew about the poisoning. Spend enough credits, and you can acquire a wide variety of information." She grinned, and I almost lost the two corn dogs I'd crammed down. "But now? This is all me." She leaned in and whispered, "Just sleep now. Close your eyes and sleep."

As the fog closed in around my mind, I realized why Mrs. Gol had been rubbing my back. Clever little piece of…

9

Don't Judge a Book
by Its Cover

My eyes fluttered open to darkness, but I didn't need to see my surroundings to know where I was. Even after years of sitting mired in the muck, abandoned by her crew, the antiseptic smell of a medical bay lingered—that, or the *Rapscallion* owners had pumped in the unmistakable aroma for the tourists.

"Cain?" I struggled to sit up but couldn't—not from a lack of physical ability but because of the restraints covering my body.

I screamed, bloodcurdlingly fearful and furious. Small spaces aren't great for me. The hab-unit on the *Starshine* barely passed acceptable levels. At least in that cramped space, I had room to move, even if only a few steps in either direction. I couldn't stand being strapped down and forcibly restricted. I was about to go into a full-blown panic attack if something didn't change within the next few seconds.

Nothing changed.

My chest tightened, my breaths becoming shallow and rapid. Heat rushed to my cheeks, and I thrashed against my bonds. They wouldn't budge. The smell of the room overwhelmed me, its scent blossoming into a full-blown headache and a stomach full of regret at downing those corn dogs.

"Cain! Help, someone!" I cried over and over until my voice grew hoarse and my tears dried and crusted against my cheeks.

I screamed inwardly, hoping Cain was close enough to pick up on my distress. What if the telepath trick didn't work over great distances? Surely enough time had passed for him to realize I'd disappeared. Cain was vexing, no two ways around that, but would he leave me? The IGJ wanted me alive, so wouldn't he have to follow orders?

The panic attacked all my reasoning. Logic twisted in on itself. What if he was the assassin? What if Cain had killed the real IGJ agent and taken their place in a clever attempt to glean what I knew before taking me out?

Yet the second time, the assassin hadn't poisoned me. Mrs. Gol had. But maybe Cain had known her plans all along, which circled back to telepathy. If he could read my mind, shouldn't he have been able to read hers? Maybe Mrs. Gol had practice in keeping her mind closed. But Cain hadn't fussed over her waiting and going on the tour with us. He'd hardly protested before leaving me to go get water.

If that was the case and he was the assassin, he would've been able to wipe his hands clean of my whole situation. Cain could go back to his employers, tell them the target had been eliminated, and have no fear of anything tracing back to him.

But what about Mrs. Gol? What was her motive? Had I been right? Was she a purist? Or was she out to take retribution against a traitor's daughter?

As endless scenarios danced through my imagination, the lights flared to life. The abrupt departure of the darkness forced me to squeeze my eyes shut, and I fought to open them against the glare of one particularly bright lamp overhead.

"Did you enjoy your nap, dear?"

I really would have preferred that Mrs. Gol morph into some hideous flesh-eating monster like the Farle from the Pilari sector. The Farle were winged predators with bulbous, rotten-smelling flesh on their head, neck, and chest. Their feathers were the revolting color of olive-green slime and, in the numerous pictures I had seen, were frequently tinged with the blood of their prey. Farle intelligence was heavily debated in academic circles. The minority argued for recognition on the sentience scale established a few hundred years prior. They pointed to evidence of loose social constructs and awareness of self from the few recorded survivor reports.

The majority of academics argued against sentience recognition, preferring to keep the Farle labeled as a dangerous predator, which emboldened trophy hunters and random attempts at eradicating the Farle in order to colonize their world.

So if Mrs. Gol had shifted into something along the

lines of a Farle, I could understand its basic predator instincts. I would brush off my fear, just as someone does after spending the evening huddled under a blanket, watching a horror movie. Monsters were supposed to come in the package of something hideous, not sugar-coated in the skin of a seemingly benign little old lady.

I refused to answer and let out one last hoarse cry for help.

Mrs. Gol had the audacity to cluck at me. "Child, do you think I would go to all this trouble and not anticipate your screams? Shields, screens, and comm blocks are all easily accessible tech these days."

I snapped my mouth shut and glowered.

Mrs. Gol carried on. "This turned into a happy circumstance, you winning the voucher for the cruise. I had planned on something similar myself, but when I was told what had happened, it was nice I wouldn't have to spend the credits."

If I was going to survive, I had to push past my fear. Turning my attention to Mrs. Gol bustling back and forth in the room, I forced myself to take deep, even breaths. Whatever the lady had planned, I would stay alive. I would get through this ordeal.

"I'm so glad you were able to save some credits," I responded, laying the sarcasm on thick, like the Tri-cLath pudding. "I would hate to see you waste them."

That earned a chuckle. "How thoughtful of you."

"So, to what do I owe this honor?"

I thought keeping her talking might be good, possibly

distracting her from whatever she was doing. It would be a good distraction for me, that was for sure.

"Oh, you just wait and see. It's a surprise." She turned and grinned, which made my stomach roll. "I've been planning this for quite some time."

"Just yourself? Seems like a lot of work."

"Oh, indeed. Thankfully, you've helped make some of it easier. Those assistance bots? I would've had to risk using my Grav' No More boosters to get you here if you hadn't needed those."

Great. Thanks, potential assassin, whoever you are. Isn't it fantastic when the plans of all the people trying to kill you come together like that? Just thrilling. I'll have to be sure to send them all a thank-you note.

"So, what's the plan? Everything going to happen here?"

Mrs. Gol waved a dismissive hand. "Oh, no. We're waiting for the tours to finish for the day, then we'll pick up where we left off."

"Won't they come looking for us?" I asked with a small spark of hope.

Desmo Voro Starshine Adventures might not be the best, but they wouldn't want to report losing some of their guests. That would be bad for business.

"No. I discussed your situation with the captain, and he knows how terrible you're feeling and that I've arranged for private transport home. He does send his condolences at not being able to finish the rest of the cruise."

Saturn's rings. Should've seen that coming.

If she was planning on moving me, that would have to be my opportunity. The assistance bots were clumsy and refused to acclimate to my biomechanics despite my fiddling with them. But I could use that to my advantage, feigning defeat and acquiescing to Mrs. Gol's demands then tripping or something. I could knock her to the ground and immobilize her. I felt sure the only way that was going to happen was with a good swift kick to the head.

Honestly, the idea was quite satisfying.

To my horror, Mrs. Gol began to hum. The medical bay provided excellent acoustics, and her robust alto voice floated throughout the room. The melody caught my attention, and I swore I knew it. But for the life of me—no pun intended there, folks—I couldn't place it.

"Shouldn't be too much longer, dear. The final tour will be finished in a few moments. Then it's about an hour till shutdown and the tour employees head off to their quarters."

I realized I'd been asleep far longer than I thought. That meant if Cain was going to rescue me, he would've done so already unless my earlier panic-driven theories panned out. Or—a new one suddenly wedged in between the others—what if Mrs. Gol had done something to him as well? At that point, I wouldn't have put it past her.

She resumed her humming, the tune soon annoying me as I couldn't figure out where I'd heard it before. So instead, I tried to think about different ways I could take her out and leave that cursed ship. It would certainly be a problem, and I came to the conclusion that I would have to hole up somewhere until the next round of tours began. And I had no idea when that was going to happen. Stupidly, not having researched that little trip before or after Mrs. Gol had informed me, I had ignored anything to do with it.

I deeply regretted that decision.

I didn't know how often groups stopped for tours and highly doubted they happened every day. Who in their right mind would come all the way out to Quarter's Landing, spending money to see this ship? Raving-mad lunatics, that's who. I was confident they came only every few weeks or months, meaning my chances of finding help or safety with the next tour were slim to none.

Hold the reactor core. Mrs. Gol had commented on the tour employees going off to their quarters. I bet they were larger than my hab-unit on the *Starshine*. Anywho, if I could figure out where those quarters were, maybe I could find an employee who would help. Better yet, according to ChowHo Insurance, there would have to be emergency transport ships somewhere close by. Most ships sported a basic AI interface with emergency override protocols in case the pilot was severely injured. That might not have been my bailiwick, but in a pinch, I could figure out how to worm my way into the system.

"All right, dear. Looks like it's time to start getting ready."

I swear the lady bounced over to me before taking a bioscan and fiddling with the restraints.

Okay, here we go. The stage performance of a lifetime.

I snarled at her for good show. It wouldn't have been realistic if I didn't show some kind of resistance, right?

"Now, I should warn you. These lovely assistant bots have been reprogrammed and are at my disposal. You'll have basic motor functions, but please don't entertain any thoughts of running off. My old bones might not be able to keep up with you, but the signal has been boosted, and I can simply shut the bots down."

"Fine," I snapped. "You win."

Mrs. Gol patted my arm, and I forced myself to relax. "Oh, it isn't a contest, dear."

With the last of the restraints gone, Mrs. Gol stepped back. "All right, let's get up off that bed now."

The difficulty I had swinging my legs to one side and pushing myself into a sitting position wasn't an act. Lack of food, lack of water, poison, and a sedative whose aftereffects were impairing the use of my arms had all taken their toll. Wrap all that up in a nice, bright package, and I wasn't even close to fully functioning.

With a deep breath, I heaved my body forward and would've crashed to the floor if not for the assistance bots maintaining my balance. My upper body swayed like an untethered weather kit in a lunar storm with each tentative step forward.

"Nice and easy. We're in no rush."

I knew I was being childish, but as she turned to unlock the door, I stuck my tongue out at her. I couldn't help myself, and it felt good.

The door slid open, and Mrs. Gol stuck her head

out. Oh, the images that ran through my head at that moment. Sigh.

Evidently satisfied that the path was clear, she turned back to me. "All right now, here we go."

Here we go, indeed, I thought.

I let my body sway as much as it could against the assistance bots, threw in a few groans for good measure, and like a drunken buffoon, I moved to the doorway. A frown formed on her face as she stepped toward me. That's it, just a few more, and I would down her like an old-fashioned bowling pin.

"I don't feel so good." I wished I could say that was acting. But I really didn't feel so great.

The frown deepened, and she stepped forward again, presumably to take another bioscan. Cue the maniacal laughter. I groaned one last time and, with all the strength I could muster, swung my right leg out to tip me off balance and crash into Mrs. Gol.

Two things happened at once.

Mrs. Gol deftly hopped to the side with an agility I hadn't considered possible, narrowly evading my rather stunning collapse, and two hooded figures appeared in the doorway.

One of the figures raised an arm obscured by its oversized robes, and Mrs. Gol stumbled back with a look of utter shock. From my luxurious vantage point on the cold metal floor, I could see a thin trickle of blood running down her chin.

Before I could thank or shrink back in terror from the next wave of nefarious individuals, one of them bent down and scooped me up. I literally mean that. I seemed not to weigh anything at all.

"Silence only now." The voice was low and full of static.

I tried to twist around to get a better look, but the only thing I realized, staring at the tightly woven blue fabric, was that my rescuers were the two Star Eaters from the cruise.

"Mrs. Gol!" I screamed as we left the medical room behind us, and I was rushed off into the depths of the *Rapscallion*.

10

A Hiccup or Two

Struggling against the iron grip of my Star Eater was useless. All I could do was wait and hope for a chance to escape. And to not be eaten. My hopes of living through the whole ordeal tanked as the reality of who'd taken me sank in.

Remember when I mentioned them before? All due respect for cultural and religious differences, but they're one group I've never cared to understand. When the news reports on Star Eater activity, it's never good—all gruesome, with a hefty body count. Star Eater activity had spiked just before the advent of the Cricade Wars and tapered off a couple of years ago. Since the wars, I'd heard a few rumors concerning a dozen low-level incidents supposedly tied to the notorious group.

Heck, even if I wanted to study their group, to dig into their religious ideology, I would pretty much have to become a member. Their security protocols are on par with the Jumjul. Whatever they believe, they keep it sealed up tighter than an airlock.

But why in Pluto would they have wanted me? I

hadn't figured them for hired assassins, but I realized that would actually make a lot of sense. What a fantastic cover for an organization of assassins. Someone always died around them, and nobody had any clue as to who they were, where they maintained any bases, or what they believed in. But if that was true and the Star Eaters had picked up my contract, why hadn't they killed me on the spot? Why did they take me?

My stomach turned queasy at some of the possible answers to that question. Again, I hoped they wouldn't eat me.

As we moved through the *Rapscallion*, the corridor walls lost their sheen. Loose bolts and missing panels exposing the delicate inner workings of a spaceship became commonplace. We were far from tour land, which meant, from my earlier glance at the tour map, the Star Eaters were moving down into the lower decks of the ship. A chill ran through my body.

Down meant only one thing: the part of the *Rapscallion* mired in the swamp. Confident the tour company would've worked at stabilizing the area—or else ChowHo Insurance wouldn't have signed off on that little profit-making scheme—I relaxed a fraction of a millimeter. Regular maintenance sweeps, though? Definitely a little sketchy on that front.

My nose confirmed my suspicions. We were indeed in the swamp. The stench of rotting plant life, waste dumps, and general gunk was strong enough to permeate the metal hull of the ship. I guessed the universe needed an appropriate perfume to compliment my predicament.

The Star Eater behind mine let loose a series of

clicks and whistles, and after a pause, mine replied. I wasn't familiar with any language consisting of those verbalizations. Of course, it could've been a code or run through a destabilizer unit designed to obscure vocal sounds. Their conversation continued for a few minutes before they made another turn and stopped in front of a door that had seen its fair share of wear and tear.

My Star Eater moved to one side, and its companion waved a hand in front of the door, which slid open even though it appeared to be lacking proper maintenance.

Fantastic.

What wonders were tucked away in the bottom of a rotting ship, on a planet of chewed-up and spewed-out slime, with the most notorious figures in the universe?

Well. Huh.

Lights flickered on overhead, and the room appeared well preserved. It was rectangular, with benches and tables bolted to the floor. Along the right-hand side, food dispensers lined the wall, with a handful of recyclers tucked up underneath those. It must've been a commissary, which also meant a habitation level. That translated into lots of potential hiding spaces, with a plethora of personnel quarters to choose from, plus all the nooks and crannies peppered throughout the level, providing areas for personnel to gather and relax.

The Star Eater conversation continued as we moved toward the back of the commissary. At the last set of tables, attached to where wall met ceiling, numerous triangular strips of blue cloth extended over the seating areas.

We ducked underneath, and I couldn't help calling out.

"Cain!"

The bleary-eyed IGJ man lifted his head, blinked a few times, and promptly fell back asleep. At least my panic-fueled nightmares weren't true—well, at first glance, anyway.

My Star Eater knelt down and laid me out on a rather comfortable mattress. Despite the temptation to relax into the luxurious piece of fluff, I tried to push off and roll away. Strong but firm hands prevented me from completing the maneuver and moved down to the assistant bots' command nodes. Unfortunately, the Star Eater displayed a knack for that type of technology. Grumble. Locking the bots into an extended position made getting up and running away pretty damn hard.

"I'm really getting tired of not being spun into the loop, guys. Care to fill me in on what's happening here?"

With another series of clicks, the Star Eater stood and, without a backward glance, left.

Yup. Nothing. Nada. I know! How rude, huh?

As they left, the lights clicked off except for two air-lamp globes suspended above me. Their design illuminated the gentle blue hue of the cloth, generating the illusion of a thousand stars dancing above us. I would give the Star Eaters a few points for aesthetics. Everything kind of reminded me of something out of one of those adventure mag-ads.

So I subscribe to a few of those things. So what? Did you see the latest issue of *The Comet Chaser*? Page twenty-nine with the portable all-in-one camping unit:

all you have to do is pick your add-ons and a spooling thread of construction nanobots. It's really nifty, with no oversized luggage to haul around, just one crate of goodies. Two hours after you set the unit down wherever you want to camp, you'll have a complete site, custom built to suit your needs. When you're done, it eats itself and can be used up to seven more times. Having that kind of tech would've made a huge difference when I was a kid, and I wouldn't have had to lug around all of Pops's stuff.

Wormhole. Sorry, I told you those tend to run in the family.

All right. I was stuck in the lower half of the *Rapscallion*, conned by Mrs. Gol, stolen by Star Eaters, and sitting next to an unconscious agent from the IGJ.

I was determined to change at least one of those things.

"Cain... Cain." Annoyed at the lack of response, I sucked in a deep breath, screamed his name as loudly as possible, and pulled my body to the left.

I flopped into him like a dead fish.

He toppled over. "What...?"

Excellent. Mission success. Except that I tried to push myself up but felt so weak that all I accomplished was lying there. I did, however, have an excellent vantage point of Cain's trousers—high-quality spin-cloth from Archeron 5, dyed a deep earthy brown and flecked with hints of gold. I hadn't paid that much attention before, but that felt a little extravagant for an IGJ man. But hey, to each their own, right?

My foray into fashion was rudely interrupted by the

retching of one nicely dressed IGJ man. At least he turned his head to one side and tried to miss me.

"Come on," I muttered and tried to turn my head.

"I—" Whatever he was going to say came up in another unbecoming pile of vomit.

At least the stench of the swamp helped smother this new and inviting odor, or else the temptation to join in might have won out.

"Are you all right?" I ventured after a few moments of silence.

"I will be." A few dry heaves. "It can take time, but one of my bioupgrades reverses the majority of toxicities."

Well, color me purple. Wouldn't that be a handy little upgrade to have? I felt a little jealous given the current predicament.

"What happened? You know Mrs. Gol took me, right? That asinine little old lady had something planned for me. And I can tell you it wasn't anything pleasant like learning how to knit or play Flip Stick cards."

Being in such close proximity, I felt Cain tense.

<She's the assassin?>

I'm confident he hadn't meant to broadcast the question or the layers of guilt surrounding those words. I paused before answering and decided against adding another layer of guilt. To be fair, Mrs. Gol would've found a way to spring her trap even if Cain hadn't left, crafty, nefarious bugger that she was.

"No. I don't think so. She didn't cop to being the one who poisoned me earlier. Why go to so much trouble? She had me holed up in one of the medical bays, waiting for the tour to finish up before fulfilling whatever warped goals she'd logged in her calendar. Plus, she said she'd been planning this for a long time too."

Cain mustered enough strength to push himself back up then let me lie there for a minute too long before helping me into a sitting position.

"Then you've got multiple targets on you."

"No kidding, detective man."

That earned a harrumph.

"What happened to you? What in Pluto's name do the Star Eaters want with us?"

Cain threw me a weary look followed by a long sigh. "I went and got the water. Didn't take but a few minutes, but by the time I returned, you and Mrs. Gol were gone. At first, I thought you'd let her talk you into continuing the tour. I know she despises me, my kind." He flinched involuntarily. "I jogged through the next several sections of the tour before I realized I'd been a fool."

I bit my tongue but thought it instead. *<Of course you were a fool. You knew someone was out to get me, and you left me alone.>* Whoops. Momentarily forgot about that whole telepathy thing. "Which begs a question. I screamed for help, vocally and mentally too."

Cain threw me a nasty look. "You were drugged for quite some time."

"That's not an answer, you know."

"I was keeping tabs on the life signs. The cluster indicated the tour group was up in command, presumably finishing up. Wherever you and Mrs. Gol had gone was either out of range or obscured."

"What?"

Then it hit me. Duh. IGJ man. Confore traded heavily in security upgrades. A whole catalog was devoted to all the different buy-ins an agent or the IGJ as a whole could subscribe to. Popular choices were retinal and various overlay systems able to tap into a wide variety of channels. Up next were subcutaneous gadgets developed in partnership with Glipglow tech. I wasn't well versed in a lot of those products. Most of the Confore tech that needed to be integrated into the body was handled by my Wepli coworkers at the Help Desk.

"Then how'd you end up down here?"

"When I realized you two hadn't simply continued on with the tour, I retraced my steps and began a systematic search. Ran into the Star Eaters, and the next thing I knew, I'm down here."

"Doesn't make any sense though, does it? I mean, if the Star Eaters are the ones who took up the contract, then why not just kill me and be done with it? Why take you? Killing an IGJ agent would only lead to an investigation. I doubt they'd want that kind of exposure."

Then again, if my initial theory was right about the religious cult being a cover for an assassination group, they had a track record of not caring about the media or legal ramifications.

"I doubt the Star Eaters are the assassins," Cain said. "Whatever they gave me knocked me out. It didn't fully incapacitate me. All my upgrades are intact. Poor strategy to leave a target armed."

"Then what's going on?" My tolerance for not understanding hit a critical level. "Can you get us out of here?"

Cain grunted and stood, almost planting his hand

in the pile of vomit as his legs tremored. He looked as weak as I did given the lackluster swoosh of his tail at the near miss.

He took a few steps forward then had to sit down at a table. "My body might have purged whatever they gave me, but it's going to take a few minutes before my strength comes back."

"Can you at least get these damn assistant bots off? At this point, they're helping everybody but me."

That didn't take long, and when he was finished, one of the bots was in pieces. His strength was returning. Watching him grab hold of a bot, frustration rippling through his body as he dug in and pulled, was oddly satisfying. The equipment cracked and then broke, little pieces of its inner workings scattering across the floor around us.

"Thanks."

That came out as more of a whisper than intended as he scooped an arm under mine and lifted me up off the floor. The abrupt change in positioning forced me to lean against him. My initial assessment of a man in peak condition had been more than correct.

I blushed, then he blushed.

"Where to?" I squeaked. Then I cleared my throat and asked again in a much more dignified voice.

"Off this ship."

A thought struck me, which I should've considered before. "Think the assassin is gone? If it's not Mrs. Gol or the Star Eaters? Our cruise has long since left. Think they would have had to board and leave too?"

Things certainly weren't looking good for the cruise's

revenue stream, having multiple passengers leave at the second stop.

"Wait, do you think the *Starshine* really left?" I asked. "You're still here, and so are the Star Eaters."

"They did. Little over an hour ago. Inquiries were made. I sent my excuses for remaining behind. Official business. I doubt they care much about the Star Eaters. But staying here means you're only going to be an open target for your adoring fans."

I shot him a dirty look. Sense of humor, huh? "Maybe I should hang around just in case they want an autograph."

He wasn't amused as we made our way through the room. Rather, he was regaining his strength, while I was a wobbly mess of uncoordinated limbs leaning against his well-muscled body. Maybe I let him think I was still weak for a little longer than necessary. Annoying though he could be, I think we all can appreciate what I was going through.

Thankfully, the door wasn't rigged to any particular biosensor, and at a wave, it slid open. The area must've been clear, as Cain didn't hesitate and brought us out into the corridor. We began our ascent out of the bowels of the ship.

As my mind cleared and my strength returned, I eventually separated myself from Cain's unusually high body temperature, my curiosity at the whole situation rearing its ugly head.

"None of this makes sense. Well, I mean the assassin part probably does if we view everything from the theory of Confore assuming I was wrapped up with the

IGJ like Jorge was. But Mrs. Gol? And the Star Eaters abducting us? What's up with all of that?"

"Does it matter?"

That was a valid question. His focus was on keeping me alive, which meant finding a way out of the *Rapscallion* and off Quarter's Landing.

But what then? Would any of those crazy mysteries be solved? Or would they just continue to follow me wherever I went?

If what Mrs. Gol had indicated was true, she'd gone to great lengths to set me up. If someone put that much time and energy into something, chances were she wasn't going to just give up. I didn't particularly like the idea of Star Eaters wanting anything to do with me either. No way in a pair of black holes was I headed back to work for Confore, but I had to have a job. I doubted any employer would look favorably on a Star Eater or two showing up abruptly at work or a little old lady coming to try and kidnap me… unless I could finagle a way to work that into a resume.

No, leaving the *Rapscallion* might've been the smart choice, but it wasn't the right choice. Whatever the universe had tangled me up in, I needed to figure it out.

Cain stopped and turned to face me when he realized I'd fallen behind. "No."

I crossed my arms. "You know, I understand you might be stressed right now, but I'm not being—what did you say—uncooperative."

Even in the dim lighting of the corridor, the sparkle of emerald was visible in his eyes. Something rumbled deep within his chest, and his tail whipped back and forth at an alarming rate. "Fine." He ground out the words. "*Tell* me what's on your mind."

"I'm not leaving. Not yet. We need to figure out what's going on first."

"We?"

"It's your job to keep me alive, yes?"

"With regard to the contract out on your head, yes."

"Oh, but that doesn't translate in other matters? You know it could all be related. What if this whole Project Clear Sight thing is a lot larger than you think?"

"The odds are against that theory."

"A bit of Jumjul in there, huh?"

That struck a nerve. In one giant leap, he grabbed my arms and shoved me up against a wall. His reaction was terrifying and slightly... well... I'll stop there. His fingers dug into my arms, and his eyes were full-on emerald, two twin jewels beaming a potent mixture of rage and anguish.

"Don't ever say anything like that again."

I didn't. I wouldn't. Contrary to some people's opinion, I did know when to keep my mouth shut.

As the emerald faded from his eyes, his grip loosened, and he backed down. He stalked off down the corridor, while I stayed put. I should've known, really.

For most, the subject of mixed lineages was touchy, not just because of the growing popularity of the purist movement but because of the difficulties for those who could claim multiple-species benefits. The cost of DNA testing alone, to prove which species were a part of your ancestry, was outrageous but necessary for gaining access to areas a particular species might mark off-limits to outsiders—such as embassies or even entire planets.

From what I understood of the whole process, even claiming mixed-species DNA was a risk. Several species, not just humans, were seeing the purist movement gaining traction. But the benefits available to be claimed by the majority of species, credit streams that added up to help offset the majority of meager credit allotments, was a huge attraction.

"Come on," he growled.

My sympathy for his situation didn't change my mind, however.

"No. I need to figure out what's going on."

"Fine, get yourself killed."

"But what about the IGJ?" I called after him.

"The job's canceled." To my astonishment, Cain left, muttering something about finding another way.

Buddy, you've got a lot to learn. The only way to get through to me is to follow my lead.

Either he truly was a heartless piece of space junk, or I'd wounded him far more than I suspected. In the end, it didn't matter. I was on my own—a lesson the universe had already taught me the hard way.

11

There's No Way
I Saw That Coming

With the lower parts of the *Rapscallion* closed off, life-support systems were running at minimal, which translated into the temperature being rather cold. Not dressed for conditions outside of an optimal artificial environment, I also realized I needed a way to protect myself. I questioned whether I should run after Cain, beg an apology, and find a way off this ship.

But I couldn't. My mind spun a new set of theories and tangled itself up with the fact that everything was happening in the last confirmed place Pops had been. Surely, that was not a coincidence.

Pops hadn't believed in them. I don't think I did, either. Things happen for a reason. Most of the time, those reasons are never understood, but I think everything in the universe is woven together. Pulling one thread causes reactions through the whole tangled mess.

I cautiously made my way through the ship and, after passing a few doors, decided to see if I could scrounge up anything useful. If my understanding of the *Rapscallion*'s layout was correct, that deck held mostly personal quarters. Maybe the tour owners hadn't cared about those decks since they couldn't make money off them, and if luck held out, I might find something useful, like a coat or a weapon or food or water or a slideshow presentation neatly laying out all the unanswered questions with understandable answers. Now, that would've been awesome.

I waved my hand at a couple of doors before one slid halfway open. I stepped over and peered into the room. No lights were inside, just several dark lumps—lumps that looked suspiciously like furniture. My hunch was right—personal quarters—but I decided not to venture in. If that door malfunctioned, getting trapped inside wouldn't do me any good.

After a few more tries, I found a door that slid open as it should. It was still a risk but a more comfortable one. Besides, my free time in the corridor would come to an end. Without Cain's nifty bioupgrades to help tell me if the coast was clear, I was operating blind.

The size of the room felt generous, far larger than I would have guessed for living allotments, but the *Rapscallion* had been engineered during a time of heightened human pride, each engineer and architect outdoing the others in their bids to work on the warship. My cramped hab-unit could easily fit five times or more in that one.

A light to my left flickered to life and helped explain the shadowy lumps. Tucked up against the right side of the room was a bed, a genuine, full-sized bed. I resisted the urge to flop down and test out the mattress.

Next to the bed was a nightstand and beyond that, a small two-person couch, complete with its own end table. The next wall held two recessed areas with soft lighting suspended above what I assumed to be a wash station and a food dispenser.

Unfortunately, both had been stripped of the majority of usable hardware. That made sense because I bet the tour's management hadn't been thinking about potential assassins and kidnapping victims stuck down here. How inconsiderate. If I made it through this whole thing, I planned to write a letter to the PR department to complain.

Luck threw me a few crumbs, though. Up against the wall, to the left of the door, stood a tall cabinet. It didn't have any security devices, so I pulled on the door and almost let out a whoop of excitement. Jackpot: two flight jackets, a jumpsuit, and a padded AV undersuit. No one cared about outdated clothing.

The temperature was dropping as nightfall approached. The padded AV suit would have provided quite a bit of warmth but also been extremely bulky and hard to maneuver in. If I got caught in a tight situation, which I had no doubt would come, it would've been more of a hindrance than a help. The jumpsuit, on the other hand, was a lighter material, and though definitely two sizes too large, it would fit over my own and at least give me another layer all over my body.

When I zipped up the jumpsuit, the smell of musty swamp assaulted me, and after questioning my life choices, I grabbed one of the flight jackets. It did add awkward bulk to my upper body, but in a pinch, I could ditch it. At least the jacket would help keep me warm in the meantime.

The rest of the room was fairly bare and didn't hold anything easily fashioned into some type of weapon. Bolts secured the furniture to the floor. The clothing bar in the cabinet was also annoyingly well constructed and firmly bolted. Someone would need a lot more strength than I possessed to get it free… or a handy set of tools.

I had a decision to make. No doubt, the Star Eaters wouldn't stay away from their captives for too long. I had no idea what they would do when they discovered our escape. Would they start searching? Abandon their plans and give up? The safe bet laid money on the idea that they sported bioupgrades of their own, enhancements that would work against little old me.

And what of my so-far-unknown assassin? Or Mrs. Gol, for that matter? The Star Eaters had dealt her a mighty blow, but I had no proof she'd actually died. She was probably going to be the most tenacious of everyone gunning for me. Maybe she wasn't the deadliest, as I would put the assassin at the top of that list, with the Gruesome Death Award going to the Star Eaters.

I settled on several facts. I needed water, and I needed food. I also needed help. Plus a weapon. All of that meant I needed to make my way back to the tourist level of the ship, break into a vendor's station, and find the crew's quarters. Shouldn't have been too hard, right?

Uh-uh. Easier planned in the head than put into practice.

Having no choice, I took a deep breath and braced as the door slid open before me. My ears strained against the silence of the corridor. At once, I feared both what I might hear and how the absence of useful noise made me feel small and vulnerable.

I had to move. I needed help. Gritting my teeth, I reminded myself that this situation wasn't any different from one of Pops's little teachable moments. He'd ensured I learned the hard way what disobeying his orders meant. Oh, I cried buckets of tears those first few times I got myself lost, wandering through ancient alien ruins, searching for him. Each time, I would miraculously find my way back to our campsite, Pops and my brother always waiting for me.

He would reach out, lift me up onto his lap, and wipe away my tears. While he reassured me I was safe, he would admonish me for not listening. I learned the hard way to pay attention to what he said. When I was a little older, with a few more years of understanding under my belt, I grew mad at what he'd done and yelled at him that I could've died, that I was no more than a kid and his responsibility.

I don't know if I wore him down or he'd simply gotten mad in return and spilled the secret. I'd never been in harm's way. He'd had a tracker sewn into my clothing and always kept tabs on where I was. Honestly, that made me even madder until the night the Howlers came.

I shivered. That was a memory I didn't want to remember anywhere, let alone in the abandoned hull of the *Rapscallion*. Pops had known what he was doing. He was raising two kids in dangerous environments, and he couldn't have us relying on him or technology to see us through. Too many times, technology failed, and those dependent upon it found themselves straight out of luck.

The next intersection gave me only one option. Time to head up to the next deck. Having been frightened out of my gourd when the Star Eaters took me, I wasn't sure how many decks down I was. I hoped I would hit something useful soon.

I shouldn't have thought that.

Even in the dim lighting, their shadows appeared seconds before their voluminous robes. Without any great options, I retraced my steps as quietly and quickly as possible and slipped back into where I'd borrowed the clothing. Ducking down behind the wardrobe, I held my breath.

The walls weren't built for privacy. A series of clicks and whistles was audible even through the reinforced rithnoleum-steel construction. I had no complaints. If I could hear them, my timing for a mad-dash exit improved.

Their unique vocalizations grew faint as the Star Eaters moved past my location, and I decided to give myself a count of sixty before making a run for it. I started the silent countdown and strained for any sound telling me they hadn't moved on. Nothing. No clicks or whistles, soft footfalls, or any indication they were still out there. A weapon would've been really useful right then.

The countdown complete, I gave the room one last sweep, and my eyes rested on the nightstand. After tip-toeing over to it, I pulled open the top drawer and, to my delight, was able to wiggle it free. Was the drawer a great option? Nope. But it was an option, at least something that could land a blow if need be and potentially give me a few seconds' head start.

Time to go. The door slid open when I approached, and I held the drawer aloft, ready to swing. The corridor was empty. I stepped out, looked in both directions, and didn't waste any time. Jogging, my breath coming in audible rasping gasps, the doors flew past until I found myself back at the intersection.

That time I didn't stop. No need to. I knew where I had to go.

But I should have. Hindsight is always twenty-twenty.

You guessed it—the Star Eaters. Those crafty little dermatex droppings must have realized where I'd hidden and doubled back.

I backed up as quickly as I could, my nightstand drawer held aloft, just waiting for one of them to come at me.

"Indulge forgiveness, offspring of the humanoid Wats Hawking Orion."

That was a combination of words I hadn't seen coming.

"Excuse me?"

"Does the offspring of the humanoid Wats Hawking Orion lack comprehension?" the other Star Eater asked.

"Excuse me?" seemed to be the only words I was capable of at the moment.

The two hooded figures exchanged a brief series of clicks and whistles before turning their attention back to me.

"Inadequate exchange between t-square and reader must have occurred," one of the Star Eaters said.

I started to say it again then snapped my mouth shut. T-square? Did they just say that?

"What do you know about it?" I asked.

Had Cain been lying all along and working with… the Star Eaters?

"Did the offspring of Wats Hawking Orion not initiate the t-square and view its message?" one of the Star Eaters asked.

"You bet your shiny rockets I did. But what's that got to do with you?"

Simultaneously, they took a step toward me.

"Uh-uh. You stay where you're at." I waved my vicious-looking box at them.

"It was foretold. It was a warning for the offspring of Wats Hawking Orion." They spoke in unison this time. Creepy vibes were all around me.

The old synapses fired, and my jaw dropped. "You slipped the t-square into my pocket? When? How? Good grief, I thought it had been Cain and typical IGJ secrecy and all that."

"We did not account for potential disruptions to the Celestial Ray," one of them said.

The questions and confusion just piled up. "Stop. First of all, why? Why did you do it?"

"A Vow upon the Celestial Plain must not be forsaken," the other Star Eater answered.

"Right, life-altering answer there. Try again. Why did you give me the warning?"

After a few clicks, they said in unison, "A Vow between those of the Celestial Light and Wats Hawking Orion."

Clear as waste fuel.

"You knew Pops?"

"He was vibrant to those of the Celestial Light," they answered.

"I don't buy it. Why would my Pops have anything to do with Star Eaters?"

Their cringing was obvious even under the heavy cloth of their robes. Interesting. They didn't like the name popular media had given them. Too bad.

"This is not a place of discussion. We fulfill our Vow to Wats Hawking Orion and turn you away from this Ray of Absence." The answer came from one of the pair.

They began to walk toward me, and I was ready to swing.

"Please. No fear. The danger ahead is not for you." They spoke in their eerie unison voice again.

"Oh, it most certainly is." I'd met all the danger before me, Mrs. Gol and the two Star Eaters. "Back off. None of this makes sense, and I'm not going to put any trust in the two of you."

My first thought was that they were lying. If they'd researched the manifest, they knew who I was and could've been tossing Pops's name around as bait, which circled back to the same old question: what did any of these psychos want with me?

"It is foretold," one said.

"The Vow remains unbroken. Offspring of Wats Hawking Orion, you must see with the Eye of Radiance," the other added.

"Thanks, but no thanks," I said.

"We carry no harm for your form. The Vow remains unbroken," they said.

"I said back off."

They subtly crept forward, and I backed up with every nonsensical sentence they spewed.

"It is of no matter. You must see with the Eye of Radiance."

Together, the Star Eaters bowed and, to my astonishment, turned and disappeared down the corridor. What in the nine celestial bodies had just happened?

To say the whole experience was bizarre would've been the understated fact of the year, probably of a lifetime. My spike of adrenaline at the abrupt appearance of the two robed figures waned. I lowered my shaking arm, forced myself to take several deep breaths, and realized the Star Eaters had actually made me creep up the ramp to the next deck. I wasn't sure what to think about that.

Pressing myself against the wall, I listened, working to keep my breathing even and slow. Nothing sounded out of order, no low murmurs or the soft padding of feet. I took a deep breath. The stench of the swamp wasn't as strong, telling me I was close to tourist land. I didn't take any more chances and glanced around the corner, noting the lights getting a tad brighter. The corridor was empty.

A handful of times in my life, I'd wished I'd gotten a few of the bioupgrades Confore offered their employees at a deep discount. Right then was in my top ten. The Retinal Deluxe Package sounded wonderful. It came with heat sensors, bioscanners, and full-spectrum analysis, and for a few more credits, a user could upgrade to a display unit hooked directly into their neural net. The nifty piece of tech allowed the user to overlay information and queries in their field of vision without anyone else knowing what was going on.

But all I had were my God-given senses and my gut.

My gut told me the coast was clear. I stepped out from the wall and continued my way up the ramp.

My gut had lied.

I bolted back around the corner so quickly that even a speed-stalker couldn't have caught me. No way was what I saw possible. Taking a deep breath, I peeked around the corner. Yup, it was still there—something that definitely shouldn't have been.

A few meters up the ramp stood a military officer. Oh, I know what you're thinking: hooray, there's help, and all is good.

Nope and more nopes. Mrs. Gol might have memorized the standard tour bull, spun to make people buy commemorative knickknacks and spread the word about their mind-blowing time on the *Rapscallion*, but I knew the real history of the behemoth.

Military uniforms usually changed due to public sentiment, fashion trends, and practicality in respect to technology and training upgrades. The dress code during the time of the *Rapscallion* was unique, specifically designed for that class of ship, and presently deemed a relic, as the uniforms had been ditched along with the designs for its sister ships.

The military officer blocking my way was wearing the deep purples of command, complete with calf-high boots, fitted dress jacket, and a hard-wired comm-sleeve.

The comm-sleeve, paired with a cranial dataport, was a dead giveaway for the time and style of uniform.

The introduction of a comm-sleeve paired with a cranial dataport had been a revolutionary design, green-lighted for a trial run with the command personnel aboard the *Rapscallion*. If ever there was a commercial advocating against integrated biotech, those things were it. They were notorious for bugs in the first few years of use, and the original lab rats wound up fused to the things. The military pushed ahead, touting the benefits of linking directly to ship functions as a game changer. Soldiers didn't need to find a communications node or a workstation for ship updates or inputting commands because they carried that ability with them. That all sounded good on paper, but the body couldn't handle that many biointegrations, as it turned out.

Think, Mahia, come on. Command personnel? Impossible. After the Cricade Wars ended, the *Rapscallion* was recognized for her final act of bravery, with all crew and personnel shipped off to serve elsewhere. This wasn't an active ship. This was an old piece of junk, wasting away in the muck and mire of a swamp, its only purpose to suck the credits out of unsuspecting tourists.

Second of all, whoever was standing in my way was young. The youngest command-level personnel had been in their midforties. Due to all the complications of the command sleeves, none of them could've had life enhancements, not to the extent of barely aging since having served aboard the ship.

Was someone dressed up like command? Perhaps an employee was forced to dress that way for the tourists?

That seemed a much more likely answer. If so, that meant I was wrong and you were right, and help was just around the corner.

Either way, I didn't like my odds.

12

Into the Maze We Tumble

"Is someone there?"

Those stealth yoga classes moved to the top of my list of things to do after my whole ordeal. It's a prerequisite for anyone looking to go into corporate espionage, and that's a huge career choice right now. With the black market expanding every day, corporations are making a killing off beating their competitors to the punch.

Right, well, here goes nothing, I thought and stepped out from behind the corner. "Sorry. I got turned around and don't know where I'm at."

"This area is off-limits to tourists and employees. We can't be held accountable for any accidents that may occur beyond the areas indicated on the tour map."

I shrugged and tried my best at a winning smile. "No problem. Got turned around and separated from my group. Any chance you could help me out?"

"The ship is currently closed and running through a shutdown cycle until the next scheduled tour. Please head to the exits and prepare for transfer."

"That's great and all, but I don't know where any of

that is. Perhaps you could point me in the right direction. Or better yet, tell me where some food is at." I threw in a chuckle for good measure.

"The ship is currently closed and running through a shutdown cycle until the next scheduled tour. Please head to the exits and prepare for transfer."

"Right. Heard you the first time, buddy." I took a step closer and frowned. "I'm a tourist who got lost, and I need some help. Think you can?"

As the officer repeated himself for a third time, my frown deepened, and though it was foolish, I walked up to him. The officer turned to face me, not by taking a step as his body made the necessary adjustments. No, he literally rotated on the spot.

For crying out loud.

I should have realized.

Mrs. Gol had made a huge deal out of the new holographic installations. That whole horror show had slipped my mind because we hadn't reached the part of the tour where they were in operation. Yet the brains in charge must've peppered projectors throughout the ship if one was showing up there. They were probably for future budget cuts. Why maintain employees you had to pay credits to when you could use those nifty buggers?

Emboldened, I stepped up in front of it and waved my hand through the simulation. The hologram was a pretty darn good one—full matrix projections with real-time interaction software. Someone had paid a pretty penny for that kind of tech.

With a shake of my head, I walked on. If more subroutines were actively helping out tourists or employees, they were undoubtedly set to follow the ship's shutdown cycle. That meant the hologram wasn't going to be helpful.

After putting only a few meters between myself and the projection, I stopped dead in my tracks when someone said, "I see you."

Those are some spine-tingling words no one should ever hear, especially when being hunted by three different groups, lost inside an abandoned ship, and exhausted and hungry.

My pulse quickened, and I didn't want to turn. In fact, I couldn't turn, not with my body rooted to the spot, my eyes wildly searching for an escape route.

"Clever girl. I wouldn't have dreamed you'd team up with such unbecoming company. Nasty Star Eaters. Yet I should've expected something like that from you. After all, your father didn't have any standards."

My fear melted into anger. I knew what Pops had done, but no one insulted him. No matter what, he was still my Pops. Hands balled up into fists and eyes narrowed to slits, I whirled around.

All that faced me was the hologram.

"I'll need to have a few words with those two Star Eaters. They must be held accountable for what they did. It's going to take quite a few credits to clean up the internal damage I sustained," the hologram said with the grating, dulcet tones of Mrs. Gol.

"Good for them," I hissed.

"Now, that's not polite at all, dear."

"I don't give a damn what you think is polite or not. You tried to kidnap me and who knows what else."

"It'd make this all the easier if you hurried along now.

And don't fret—it truly is all for the best. You'll see. All you need to do is complete the tour."

"Then that's exactly what I won't be doing, thanks," I spat.

I did want answers, but whenever someone starts issuing commands, my brain flips to the opposite of what they want. So logically, I turned and stormed up the ramp to the next level. The walls gleamed from the regular upkeep, lights were still running at optimum strength, and best of all, location signs were posted for tourists not bright enough to understand a map.

If she wanted me to complete the tour, then I would meander and take my time, getting the answers I wanted my own way… while dodging a potential assassin. Well, whoever or whatever the assassin was, they would have to wait in line. I was obviously in Mrs. Gol's world.

But I wasn't going to rush headlong into her fantasy. That would've been dumb. I needed a plan first, and by "plan," I meant getting something to eat then rushing at the old woman like the fool I was.

According to the signs, general recreation areas were to the left: commissaries, lounges, training rooms, the library, and the like. Off to the right began the winding tour through officer quarters, starting with the lowest rank and ending at command personnel. Both options would eventually take me up to the main entrance.

Bet you can't guess which direction I took.

"This isn't the most expedient route to finish our tour."

I about jumped out of my skin as another hologram popped up right next to me when I headed left.

"Go away," I growled.

"If you turn here at the next junction, then—"

I didn't care to listen to the rest, and despite my exhaustion, hunger, and thirst, I took off at a jog, feeling a sense of satisfaction at leaving the hologram behind. The emotion didn't last long.

Another blasted one popped up in front of me. "You should turn here—"

Nope. I turned in a different direction. Frustration crept into Mrs. Gol's voice each time a new hologram appeared and tried to tell me where to go. You would think she would figure out I hated being told what to do. Whatever, lady. Thanks for at least telling me where I didn't want to go just yet.

By the time the fifth stupid hologram showed up, I slowed down to inspect the corridors. Some type of security system or projection nodule network had to be enabling the program. Coming to a stop, I considered the timing of Mrs. Gol's minions popping up at regular intervals.

Retracing my steps and ignoring the latest faux officer berating me for not following directions, I spotted its projector. It wasn't much bigger than my fist, tucked up in the crook of where wall met ceiling.

"I see you." I couldn't help saying as I stared up at the thing and grinned. Without wasting time, I reached down, pulled off my boot, and chucked it at the thing. My aim improved after a few tries, and on the third round, I smashed the sucker.

The small victory felt good even if it didn't mean much in the long run. No way could I destroy all the projectors, and even if I did, the station Mrs. Gol was undoubtedly working at would alert her to the damage, which would be a flashing signpost alerting her to my location.

If she knew, fine. I couldn't do anything about it.

After reclaiming my boot, I finally made my way to one of the commissaries, studiously ignoring the infuriated holograms. That room was more than double the size of the commissary the Star Eaters had taken me to. To the delight of my stomach, the food dispensers were intact.

I raced over and began hitting buttons. I didn't care what was dispensed. I just wanted something to eat.

Nothing happened.

I know, I know. I did the number-one thing I always tell my customers to refrain from: hitting the equipment. No matter what you might think, tech doesn't respond to a few well-placed punches.

I punched the machine, winced, and threw in a few salty words for good measure.

"Oh, honey, the ship's powering down, remember? Besides, you don't think they'd just hand out stuff for free, do you? You need credit authorization first."

"Float off, will you?" I yelled.

"Thought you were hungry, but if that's what you want, fine."

A few things happened in the span of a couple of seconds. I yelped, turned, and chucked the drawer at the intruder. Firing at the camera above the door, the intruder turned their head, but not enough to dodge my impromptu weapon. As the drawer hit its mark with a satisfying crunch, I realized it was Cain. The well-crafted drawer didn't fall apart but bounced off his head and toppled to the floor.

Cain reacted as any IGJ agent should. He spun around, weapon trained on me. As he realized what I'd done, his tail lashed back and forth, and he groaned.

"Whoops. Sorry," I said with an apologetic shrug. "But you shouldn't surprise someone like that."

"A drawer?"

I sniffed. "It worked, didn't it? Would've given me a few seconds to get away."

When I didn't receive a compliment on my out-of-the-box thinking, I stomped over and snatched the food from him. "I was doing fine, thanks."

Moving a suitable distance away, I took a seat, unwrapped the foil, and stared at a soggy piece of alt-pie. I wasn't sure I was that hungry, but my stomach growled at the spicy aroma, so with a show of displeasure, I ripped off a piece and popped it into my mouth.

Alt-meat isn't the best. It isn't even great. In fact, it's downright nasty—dirt cheap to make and used as a popular additive for restaurants to cut down on true meat expenses. Hailed as a wonder food, chockful of vit-mins and other multisyllabic nutritional words no one ever knew the meaning of, it made a fortune within the first few months for the company that invented it. Then their value plummeted alongside public opinion due to the taste until they found their true niche on the black market.

I wouldn't give Cain the satisfaction of visibly appreciating it, but it wasn't as bad as I'd expected. Whoever the vendor was, they'd done a great job of masking the alt-meat taste. Or I was just starving.

Cain ignored my looks of annoyance, disgust, and anger. Then he ignored my very explicit thoughts concerning his abrupt return.

Settling into the seat opposite mine, he avoided my eyes. "I need this job."

"So?"

"So"—he clenched his hands together—"I need you to come out of this alive."

"Kind of hard to do when my protection storms off and leaves me stranded, don't you think?"

His head whipped around, emerald eyes sparkling and brow furrowed. "You insulted me."

I had. I knew. But I wasn't feeling very magnanimous at the moment. "Then grow thicker skin."

Cain pushed away from the table and stood up. For a moment, I thought he was going to storm off again. To his credit, he didn't.

I didn't understand why I was feeling so confrontational. Maybe it came from being trapped on a ghost ship with people who wanted me dead and very few answers as to why. Or from how annoyed I was at the small flicker of relief at his showing up again. I'd never needed anyone before, so why should I feel grateful he was there then? Perhaps it had to do with being in the last place Pops had been known to be, where I knew he'd suffered, and I didn't like to think about it.

I'd dealt with insults my entire life, learning to grow a thick skin, to ignore the slurs and doors closed in my face when people found out who I was. People didn't like me—fine, I didn't like them either. I knew how to cope with a solitary life.

But as I watched Cain, I wondered what his story was. I could hide who I was, shop in any store I wanted, go where I wanted, and work where I wanted—well, at least up until the point a potential employer or landlord looked at my legal papers.

Cain didn't have that option. Unless he could afford a myriad of plastic surgeries, his physical appearance would give him away. I didn't know what that felt like. Guilt blossomed in my chest, and I wanted to apologize but found the words sticking in my throat.

"So does this mean you're going to help me figure out what's going on?" I asked instead.

Cain pursed his lips and stopped pacing. "Yes." He turned to face me. "On one condition."

"Oh?" I said, crossing my arms.

"You listen to what I tell you to do."

I scoffed. "Right."

Cain stormed over and slapped his hands on the table, leaning toward me. His eyes were still emerald, and I had a feeling they were going to be that color for quite some time.

"I mean it," he said. "Whoever this Mrs. Gol really is, she knows what she's doing. Gaining access to the *Rapscallion*'s controls takes skill. Real skill."

I honestly hadn't thought of it like that, but he was right. Fine, score one for Cain.

"The employees left shortly after the cruise ship pulled out of orbit. All that's left is Mrs. Gol, the two Star Eaters, myself, and you."

"You're sure?"

His tail whipped back and forth, almost slapping the sides of the table in his fury. "I'm sure," he ground out.

"Where is she then? The Star Eaters are below us, or at least they were." I chewed on the last of the alt-pie and watched him stop in the movement of tugging his vest down.

"How do you know where the Star Eaters are?"

"Um, well. Let's just say I had a little chat with them."

"A chat. With Star Eaters."

"Yup. So where's Mrs. Gol at?"

"You don't think filling me in on what transpired between you and the Star Eaters is important?"

"Nope."

Honestly, I couldn't wrap my mind around the idea that Pops had had anything to do with them. If some type of vow was involved, it was more than a casual relationship. I wasn't sure I could handle that revelation at the moment, on top of everything else.

He straightened and turned in his chair. "Fine. Mrs. Gol has been in command—best location to hack into the *Rapscallion*'s systems."

"Did a little reconnaissance?"

He growled.

I took that as an affirmative. "So, no assassins?"

"Unlikely. Even if they're operating with stealth tech, I would be able to detect them."

Should have thought of that. Thanks, IGJ.

"Great. So, though we're—"

The room went dark then red.

Mrs. Gol's voice came over the internal comms. "I'll

ask politely one last time. Mahia, it's time to finish the tour."

I had no time to provide a well-crafted, balanced reply as Cain bounded over the table, crashed into me, and pinned me to the ground. At least he was taking his role as protector seriously, if a little on the dramatic side.

"Get off me," I mumbled into his chest.

"We do this the hard way," Mrs. Gol said.

An automated voice took over. "This is not a drill. Report to battle stations. Intruder alert. Intruder alert."

The message continued to repeat itself as Cain got up and grumbled, "This just got a lot less fun."

"No kidding," I snapped.

He held out a hand, and I eyeballed it. But even though the alt-pie had given me a boost, I knew I wasn't at peak physical condition. Mrs. Gol's sedative had thrown me for a loop.

I slipped my hand into his and couldn't help but note how strong it felt. As his fingers closed around mine, I experienced something unexpected. Warmth flooded my body, and my head snapped up to stare at him in wonder. Now, I know what you're thinking, but the warmth wasn't that kind of warmth. The sensation was something completely different.

Have you ever experienced the feeling of stepping into a patch of sunlight, its soft rays full of life, right before it dips below the horizon? Somehow, the light illuminates everything around you, and for a brief moment, the universe is bathed in its brilliance.

That's what I felt, and I saw it reflected in the warm glow of Cain's eyes, turned amber.

Without ceremony, he hauled me to my feet and flung my hand away, the warmth leaving as abruptly as it'd come. I stood there, a little embarrassed, slack-jawed, and with only one thought: *Keep your mouth shut.* If I'd had something to say, though, I didn't. *What in Pluto just happened?*

Ignoring the whole asteroid in the room, he said, "Internal defenses should only be laser-point weapons. Any robotic defenses would have been stripped before the tours started."

"So they leave the worse option, then?"

Cain nodded. He reached into his jacket and pulled out a small handgun. I had been wrong. He hadn't smuggled a weapon on board. He'd smuggled multiple weapons on board.

Thanks to Pops, I had a basic working knowledge of most handheld weapons. I took the offered Raptor series, XS-52, and noted it came with a built-in nanobot port and slipped my hand between the grip and the main unit. The XS-52 blinked red and linked up with the chip in the palm of my hand. The light turned yellow as the weapon built an additional brace around my wrist and up the length of my forearm. The control ports opened and moved to adjust to the length of my fingers.

My thumb rested on the main control, able to toggle between Safety, Powering Down, and Armed. Each command carried its own icon projected above the thumb, reminding the wearer of the selected command. The control port underneath my pointer finger was the trigger. Only a downward motion was required to activate the weapon. The other ports could be customized, but

I turned that option off. I didn't need anything fancy, just the ability to protect myself.

Cain watched, and when I glanced up, he gave a curt nod of approval. Was that a compliment? It only irked me. What did he think I was? I wasn't fresh out of the genetic lottery.

"We'll take out the weapons as we move," Cain ordered.

"Sorry to burst your bubble, but not possible."

"Why?"

I wasn't a weapons technician, but I'd spent a fair amount of time studying the *Rapscallion*. "Embedded targeting and firing systems covered with faux paneling. If you've got an intruder in your house, would you make it easy for them to take out your defenses?"

"Fair point," Cain grumbled.

"We'll just tap-dance our way to Mrs. Gol," I quipped. When I didn't receive the appropriate chuckle, I added, "It's a human thing, an ancient expression."

"I'm familiar with it," Cain remarked.

"Oh? Ever study it?" That was something I would pay money to see.

Cain ignored me.

"Fine, spoilsport. I'm ready. Let's go crash Mrs. Gol's little party."

The quiver of his lips and a deep frown were his unhappy acknowledgment. You would think an agent with the IGJ would be more inclined to want answers than to run away with his tail tucked between his legs. Okay, I'll admit, that was perhaps a little unkind. To his credit, he kept saying he wanted to keep me safe, and my need for confrontation certainly didn't line up with that wish.

"The only way to finish this is to play by her rules. Give her what she wants. Nonessential areas will be shut down with the security alert, and any maintenance hatches will be sealed off too."

"Right, so no alternative way to sneak up on her."

"No."

"Let's get this over with."

I let Cain take the lead. Oh, no—don't start. I might keep a few tricks up my sleeve, but no matter how much he irked me, he was IGJ. It was his show. No matter what his ranking might have been, he'd gone through years of training to earn that badge.

"You will stay tucked up behind me at all times unless ordered elsewhere. Move when I say so and stop where I tell you. Clear?"

"Yes, sir," I said with a mock salute.

With a deep growl, he said, "On the count of three." His tail moved in time with his countdown as the door slid open, and we headed out into the corridor.

13

This Is Not
What I Signed Up For

The ship's interior glowed with pulsating red light, making my skin crawl. Cain moved forward a few steps, eyes and weapon sweeping the area. I moved with him, barely breathing, my heart pounding. While the man was an annoying bugger, the odds of Mrs. Gol deciding to kill me and be done with it after all that trouble were next to nothing. Whatever twisted scheme she'd devised, her plan needed me alive. Cain, on the other hand, represented something she hated, which made him expendable. The idea didn't sit well with me.

We made it to the next junction without incident, and Cain motioned for me to stay put. To my own shock, I followed directions. I sucked in a deep breath as he moved around the corner, sure Mrs. Gol would activate the defenses and fire.

After a few miserably long seconds, he came back around. "All clear."

With an audible sigh of relief, I resumed my position,

eyes and ears straining to pick up on anything that would alert us to danger. Despite Cain's apparent nifty bioupgrades for that type of situation, I was well aware how easily tech could malfunction. I wasn't in the mood for a sneak attack from behind.

That day was going to be a long one.

We continued the pattern of moving together through the corridors and Cain having me wait when we came to a corner or intersection before moving on. Pretty soon, we reached the area where we'd started that nightmare of a tour.

"Are you sure?" Cain asked.

His question was valid. He didn't need to be a telepath to sense my fear and anxiety, not to mention how I still felt physically awful. Any sane person would've felt that way in the situation. But I shook my head. I wanted answers.

"Yes."

Our next stop was where the crafty little Mrs. Gol had drugged me—not by our choice, mind you.

Mrs. Gol's voice broke the silence. "I would provide a compliment on your choice to complete this tour, but my patience is wearing thin."

"Oh, what a—"

The *Rapscallion*'s internal defense system lit up and punched a series of minute holes a few centimeters from the tips of Cain's boots.

"Holy Jupiter!" I yelped and grabbed Cain, yanking him back. We tumbled to the ground with Cain providing a colorful commentary on my attempt to save his life. Untangled and unharmed, I scowled at a hologram that had popped up beside us. "Cutting it a little close, aren't you?"

"Yes, well, I'm afraid we'll have to expedite the process now, and I had so many wonderful things for you to do too. Pity." The hologram gave us a stiff bow and extended an arm, indicating we should turn left.

"We'll see about that," I grumbled. Picking myself up, I stomped off to the right and earned another round of fire. "Really? So that's how you're going to play it?"

The hologram smirked. Cain attempted to move back the way we'd come, but Mrs. Gol made it quite clear we could safely move in only one direction.

"Remind me to steer clear of little old ladies in the future," I muttered.

Cain threw me what I was coming to designate as his signature scowl. "Stay there."

I stayed true to myself and followed him, earning another scowl. I should've been keeping track of those things, tossing a credit into a virtual piggy bank every time or something. I might have even earned enough to take another cruise, and wouldn't that be a lark?

I'll admit that turning left was a little anticlimactic, as nothing happened. Nothing cleaved us in half or anything. We had only a few close calls whenever we made a turn Mrs. Gol didn't care for.

As we entered the deck directly below command, Cain stopped and nearly made me jump out of my skin as he fired off a few rounds, disabling the projectors and cameras.

"Give a little warning, would you?" I clutched my chest, eyes wide at the adrenaline spike.

"She might know we're here, but we should be able to talk in private for a few moments before she figures out a workaround," Cain said, ignoring my dramatics. "This is where we split up."

My brow furrowed. "What?"

"You understand as well as I. Mrs. Gol doesn't want me. She wants you."

I didn't like where that was heading.

"There's only one way up to command from here. I'll go ahead and disrupt the projectors and cameras. Give you an edge and take some pressure off."

"Pressure? How's that going to relieve any pressure?"

Cain crossed his arms. "We both know you should be in a medical bay, getting checked out."

I tried to argue. "I'm not that bad."

Cain only scoffed. "Give me twenty, then go."

I shook my head. "That's a suicide run, and you know it."

Cain blinked then tapped twice behind his right ear. "You think this is where I'm going to make my last stand in life?"

"You intolerable piece of space junk," I hissed. "You had shielding this whole time?"

He shrugged. "Why let her know before we needed to?"

I had more than a few words to say to him and his superiors. Show 'n' Tell was going to find quite a few scathing ratings of the IGJ from me. They wouldn't be morale boosters, that was for sure.

"Give me twenty," he reiterated.

Oh, no you don't, I thought. I leveled the XS-52, sighted my target, and fired.

Cain whirled around, weapon at the ready.

"Don't be a fool," I said calmly. "Mrs. Gol doesn't like you. In fact, she hates you or at least what you represent."

Cain drew in a breath, shoulders rising.

"I'm not trying to pick a fight, simply stating a fact. If you head off on your own, I'm betting she'll kill you. Sure, your death might be a long-drawn-out ordeal with your fancy-schmancy shielding. But like you said earlier, Mrs. Gol is good, whoever or whatever she really is. She'll find a way. My guess—she didn't have complete control of the system before you so generously came back to help. But she obviously has control now."

Cain stared at me with an intensity that would've made me blush if I wasn't fed up with the whole death-trap situation.

"Right, or maybe it's because of your winning personality and people skills," I muttered.

Proving my point, he just stood there and crossed his arms.

"Look, you're here to make sure I come out of this alive. That means we stick together. No more running off on your own to do who knows what, got it?"

I suspected the real reason he was eager to scamper off was that Cain wasn't a team player. I could respect that, but my gut was telling me we would be better off sticking together. "Fine."

Cain stalked past me and took the lead. "Coming?" he snapped.

"See? My point right there—winning personality."

We didn't get very far before we earned ourselves another round of fire.

"What the heck, Mrs. Gol? We're following the signs," I snapped, whipping my head around to spot the security camera.

"Yes, you are, dear, but there is one part of this tour we can't miss. Please turn to your right."

I looked over my shoulder, "What's to the ri—"

Uh-uh. I didn't want to do that. Not there. Not while being manipulated by a crazy old lady. I moved forward instead.

"Please don't do that."

I didn't care. I took another step and another.

"I will be forced to turn you around."

"Then get it over with. I'm not going in there."

"My poor child, this is something you must experience. I dealt with such a hassle when they installed this particular part of the tour. So many layers of red tape to untangle, not to mention public sentiment."

"No. I know what happened. I don't need to see it too."

"You do."

"Look, lady, I could argue with you until we both fade off into the Nethers. I'm not going—"

Mrs. Gol activated the defenses, took aim, and fired. I was all set to laugh at her fool's errand, trying to hurt Cain in order to make me go where she wanted. Little did she know. Cue a victorious round of laughter. He'd been smart to keep his shielding a secret.

I, on the other hand, was not smart.

My face froze, I imagined, in that ungainly expression someone might get right before chuckling their way out of an awkward joke. As pain bled across my left shoulder and down into my upper arm, I looked up. "You shot me?"

While my brain played catch-up with my body, Cain pulled me down, his body now shielding mine.

"Why'd you shoot me?" I asked, more than a bit flummoxed.

The answer came from behind us.

"My dear, I need you alive, yes. But that can be accomplished with a wide variety of tools left onboard as colorful displays for the tourists. If you continue to play the ungrateful child, then I shall be forced to take appropriate steps to ensure you comply. Though this is all an entirely disgraceful situation, I'm quite certain your companion doesn't want you dead. Do you, Turen ed-Suren Heron?"

Well, excuse my language, but shit. So much for secrets and surprises.

We'd been hers to toy with the entire time.

"I noted your recent dip in ranking among IGJ agents. Adding yet another unsolved case to your file wouldn't be good, would it? They might even relegate you to hazmat sweeps. Do you think it's a failure on your part, due to your unfortunate breeding, or some unfair hand the universe has dealt you?"

I twisted around, ready to defend Cain, only to find an image of a man in his sixties speaking with Mrs. Gol's voice, his skin wrinkled from too many years spent in the elements, hair whiter than the snow on

Mandarin's Rhine, and clothed in the tatters of an explorer's jumpsuit.

If anything in the universe was ever unholy, it was her singsong voice coming from the hologram of my pops. I experienced two distinct reactions. The first was revulsion. I shrank away from the abomination into the solid warmth of Cain's body. A hand moved to rest on my uninjured shoulder, and for a brief moment, I took comfort in the unsolicited gesture.

When the only-too-real image of Pops smiled, rage roared to life inside me. Without thinking, I raised the XS-52 and fired round after round, watching them pass through the hologram to damage what lay beyond.

Cain's hand slid down my arm, over the Raptor's brace, and covered my fingers with his own. I didn't want to stop. I wanted the hologram destroyed. I wanted to destroy Mrs. Gol for what she was doing. If she wanted to play games with me, fine, but she had no right to defile my Pops's image or memory.

His fingers pressed against mine, forcing my trigger finger to curl back, and he pressed his thumb against the control port to power down the weapon. I spun around and buried my face in his chest, trying to refuse the tears threatening to spill over. Cain's hand moved to cup the back of my head, and for a moment, he held me tightly.

"If you don't get Mahia to complete this part of the tour, I find I will have no option but to fire upon her again. And again. Until she sees what she needs to see and is then brought to command. Do you understand, consultant, who needs to keep her alive?"

I felt Cain's muscles in his chest move as he nodded.

"Don't do this," I breathed against him.

"We have no choice."

"There's always a choice. I don't want to see this. I don't want to play her game. You were right. Just get us out of here."

Cain pulled back, and I expected to see frustrated emerald eyes staring down at me. Instead, I found myself lost in a sea of crystallized amber, an intensity of light blazing from within. "I won't let her hurt you."

But she will, I thought, *in more ways than any ship's defense system could accomplish.*

Reluctantly, I allowed Cain to help me to my feet.

"A moment, Mrs. Gol." Cain laid something warm against the wound.

Within a few moments, I felt the sting of antiseptics and the tingling of a tissue-regeneration patch. When finished, Cain turned me toward the hologram. I looked everywhere but at its face.

"Very good. On with the tour." The pleasure in the woman's voice made me want to reach through the ship and throttle her.

The door opened, and after a quick sweep of the area, Cain ushered me into the Central Processing Unit for the *Rapscallion's* prisoners.

14

Central Processing

Lights fluttered to life as we entered, illuminating a crescent-shaped desk centered between two smaller square desks a meter or so from the main unit. View screens cluttered the walls, their blank faces watching us as we took a few more steps into the room.

The hologram of Pops moved with us and spoke, not with the voice of Mrs. Gol, thank Jupiter, but of a man with a raspy tenor. The voice wasn't my pops's. His had been deep, rich, and smooth, able to craft wonder out of thin air.

"Welcome to the *Rapscallion's* Central Processing Unit. This innovative design is a departure from contemporary military ships. Most brigs or cells for enemy combatants or personnel were located away from command. In an effort to emulate the Jumjul, the architects designed this ship with the brig located next to command. The reasoning behind this was ease of access to prisoners for interrogations and strengthened security measures inherent in command level."

"Don't forget the Jumjul are a tad on the arrogant

side too," I muttered. I suspected the Jumjuls' real reason was to flaunt their military prowess against their enemies rather than anything practical, despite the best reasons humans had invented to justify emulating them.

"A prisoner would be escorted by ship's security to Central Processing. Biodata would be uploaded into the computer's system, where all bioupgrades would be rendered useless and appropriate confinement assigned. This accomplishment came about with the newly minted damping field, coupled with an AI processing unit able to extend the field over target areas exclusively." Pops's avatar moved to the center of the desk, and a screen flared to life.

"Would any of our guests be interested in experiencing this interactive station? Pictures and replays can be purchased at Ithia's Photobooth two decks below us once your tour is complete."

No, thank you. But I was sure more than a few would eat up the opportunity. A good handful of parents probably wouldn't mind a few minutes of peace and quiet while their kids experienced the *Rapscallion*'s security.

"If not, then please select a reenactment you'd like to see." The screen split into four different sections, images and names rotating through each one.

Mrs. Gol's voice hijacked the hologram. "There's no time to waste. Go ahead, dear. You know which one to select."

"No."

I said I was stubborn.

Cain resolved the issue by selecting the image of Pops.

My hand rubbed against my collarbone, and I bit my

upper lip. I didn't want to, but when Cain extended his hand, mine fell into his, and together, we followed the hologram down into a part of my life I'd always known I would have to confront at some point. I just hadn't guessed the moment of confrontation would happen in this manner.

The hologram's preprogrammed voice didn't return as its character structure shifted. Dead eyes stared past us, and Pops's image appeared to collapse in on itself, representing a man defeated and at the end of his life. Tears stung my eyes at seeing him that way, even if the image had been programmed by some distant corporation hoping to make money off his torment.

"My name is Wats Hawking Orion."

A million memories came flooding back at the sound of his voice, each one ripping through me like debris tearing through the hull of a ship with no protective shielding.

"The *Rapscallion* officers arrested me toward the end of the Cricade Wars. Charged with treason against humanity, I was brought to trial through the InterGalactic Justice system. My crimes"—as if hearing the charges wasn't enough, an info screen popped up to list the crimes as well—"stand as providing the Eeri military with strategic information concerning humanity's military and our allies. This intel provided the Eeri the locations of over fourteen different outposts, stations, and ships, all subsequently attacked. I was charged with the murders of over three thousand people."

That was public record. I'd read through the reports more than a dozen times, searching for anything out of place or a clue my pops might have left. But though I knew all that by heart, each word still delivered a venomous sting.

The hologram shifted, and three more appeared around it. I recognized Captain Uriku Tow. Despite the disgrace and unpopular public sentiment she'd endured, the last-minute victory against the Eeri had catapulted her into popular history. Her face was commonly emblazoned on IGJ pamphlets, her biography used to entice sign-ups for the military. A woman of few words but keen military strategy, she'd been raised on Usuler's moon, the daughter of agricultural workers, and her rags-to-riches story spawned fans across the worlds.

The architects of the program had been allowed to craft a less-than-stellar image of the woman, which was surprising. The hologram bore dark circles under her eyes, with a weary but determined expression.

"It never had to be this way, Wats. You know it, and I know it," Captain Tow stated as the hologram crossed her arms and nodded at the security guards.

Strong hands clamped down on my arms, preventing me from rushing forward. I struggled against Cain's strength for a few moments, my instinct to help defend Pops overwhelming. Deep down, I knew I couldn't do anything, but the desire didn't go away. Tears streamed down my face as I watched them beat Pops, sweeping his legs out from under him and landing blows on his back, head, and limbs.

During the height of the Cricade War, the ban on unethical interrogation techniques was lifted when it became painfully apparent that humanity and its allies were losing. The hologram program was showing nothing compared to the horrors I'd read about.

Schematics for bioupgrades were frequently commandeered and twisted into tools of horror in order to pry information out of prisoners. Multiple books, academic reports, and newscasts had dedicated time to uncovering the atrocities sanctioned. Public sentiment fell into two camps, those who agreed with the ruling and those who believed the ban should've stayed. The Old Earth Monarchy is still doing a clean-up job on its image after the reports came out and it reinstated the ban.

Knowing what the program wasn't showing, each kick or blow made my guts twist as I felt the sting of everything they weren't showing. How could any tourist come and witness this? Did they get a sick joy out of it? How many would ever stop and think about the man he'd been, the family he'd had?

"That's enough," Captain Uriku Tow snapped. Her image crouched down next to Pops. "Tell us why. What information did you provide? What's the Eeri's next move?"

Pops's hologram voice picked up the narrative as the captain stood, nodded at her security, and turned a blind eye as they continued their assault.

My anger burned through the tears.

"Wats Hawking Orion refused to tell the captain or subsequent interrogators any information. However, security feeds, eyewitness testimony, and information gleaned from captured Eeri ships all point to this man having revealed the locations and strengths of the fleet. Later, after sentencing, new information came to light, detailing how Wats Hawking Orion was additionally suspected of providing the locations of several military installations sanctioned by the Old Earth Monarchy."

The recreation continued as the security officers lifted Pops and dragged him down to one of the containment cells. We had no choice but to follow.

As we reached the cell, a duplicate of Pops's hologram appeared. One version was sitting on the hard metal bench, hunched over with his head hanging low. His hands were limp between his legs as the duplicate stood off to one side and picked up the monologue.

"It's unknown why this man would betray his species and humanity's allies. The best the military had to offer tried to get answers, anything to understand the motivations for his defection. None were ever given. To this day, it remains a mystery, perhaps one of the greatest mysteries of our time."

I listened as the hologram rattled off several theories, all ideas I'd heard again and again. Nothing was new, nothing that would help me gain some insight into why he'd done what he did. I kept my eyes on the image of Pops, defeated and sitting in the dark. *Why'd you do it, Pops? Why'd you leave us and go help the Eeri? What could have been more important to you than your own children?*

The hologram's hands twitched. I tensed as they moved again. Both index fingers moved out and back three times. Next, his hands rotated at the wrists. That pattern repeated itself two more times, then the image interlaced his fingers, closed his hands into one large fist, and snapped them apart.

A glitch in the programming was entirely possible.

If the finger and wrist movement had continued on a loop, I would've been inclined to believe it. With the fist-and-hand snapping movement, that became less likely. When the hologram's hands remained still, I knew his gestures weren't a glitch.

Pops had always been intentional with his words and his movements. Being a xenologist had trained him to be careful. Humans primarily navigate the environment through speech, supplemented with hand gestures and involuntary responses to stimuli.

In many species, those gestures and reflexes conveyed the wrong message. Xenologists spent years training their bodies to remain neutral in all types of situations. A whole subcategory of bioupgrades was dedicated to the discipline, rerouting subconscious movements to help control the body.

Pops, not being a fan of bioupgrades or any sort of biomanipulation, had learned to control his body through sheer determination. Before he left, he'd begun training my brother and me, but that was something I'd never worked on since.

If those movements were intentional, then it was a message. But to whom? Surely, someone watching or later combing through the footage would've picked up on it. Maybe they'd sloughed it off as just a doomed man biding his time. Everyone had wanted him to confess, to provide a verbal statement as to why he'd betrayed humanity. Perhaps no one had considered other ways to communicate.

The hologram's diatribe paused. It turned and flashed a smile. "If you're interested in learning more about the life and betrayal of Wats Hawking Orion, the *Rapscallion*, or the Cricade Wars, I suggest visiting Blue Bear's Books. You'll find the unauthorized biography of Wats Hawking Orion, along with out-of-print resources diving into the life of this man. If you want to replay this presentation again or wish to view another, please proceed back to the lobby of the Central Processing Unit. Thank you for visiting the *Rapscallion*."

"How dare they," I hissed, my momentary revelation forgotten.

"This is public record. They can do what they want with it," Cain stated.

I shook my head and twisted out of his grasp. "This is public record, sure. But the books… There isn't supposed to be anything published about Pops. I paid my lawyers a fair amount of credits to make sure everything was pulled and destroyed and future publications stopped."

"You can't stop a curious mind, dear. You should know that," Mrs. Gol's voice interjected.

I wanted to find Mrs. Gol and punch her in the face. "They've no legal right. I made sure of that." I was seething inside. "And frankly, neither do you. You commandeer this ship for what? To make me see what I already know about my Pops? Does this give you a kick in the pants?"

"I suppose you'll just have to come up to command and find out," she responded in her singsong voice.

"And if I don't?"

She sighed. "I do believe we've covered that already. Don't be so tiresome, dear."

I ground my teeth together. "Fine. Let's just get this

over with. Any more side attractions along the way? I'll need to pop some popcorn first if there are."

Mrs. Gol laughed. "No, I'm afraid all the extra excursions are finished. It's time to come to command. Cain, if you would be so kind."

I felt him take a step toward me but fell back as I mentally flung him an image of what I would do if he touched me. *<Get out.>* Cain was smart not to argue.

With a deep breath, I lifted my arm, and as I exhaled, my thumb pressed the Raptor's main control, powering up the weapon. No one was going to make a spectacle out of Pops again. Not without the *Rapscallion*'s owners forced to shell out a mountain of credits to rebuild their horror show.

My arm shifted, and I aimed at the bench where the hologram of Pops had sat. I fired, slowly and methodically at first, until all the grief, anguish, uncertainty, and hate were too overwhelming.

Tears streamed down my face as I screamed at Pops, at the men and women who had captured and tortured him, at the horrific display of pain people considered entertainment. How could he have left my brother and me? For what? Did he have any idea of how horrible our lives would become because of his decision to help the Eeri?

I backed down the corridor where the officers had dragged Pops to his cell, leaving nothing but smoldering piles of twisted metal. When I reached the entrance to Central Processing, my voice grew hoarse as I destroyed everything.

I had finally learned what had happened to Pops,

and I wanted nothing more than to burn those images from my mind. If I couldn't do that, then I could at least replace them with the memory of his torture chamber lying in a smoldering heap of ruins.

Leaving Central Processing behind, I set off toward command with a deep sense of satisfaction. Cain kept pace, silent and on alert. Honestly, I no longer cared. Each time I passed a communications node or a projector, I incinerated it. Mrs. Gol's voice tried to break in on my shooting spree, some admonishment, more than likely, but I fried each potential access point for her sickly voice to reach my ears. They were target practice, each one leading up to the final challenge. I would get my answers, then Mrs. Gol would pay dearly for what she'd done.

15

Curiosity Kills the Cat

The *Rapscallion*'s deck with the largest square footage belonged to command, with multiple decks above, all restricted to personnel with top-level clearance. Even though I'd done my fair share of digging into the ship's history, the military had done a superior job of keeping everything above command under wraps.

Viewed from the outside, the command deck was where the ship bulged slightly outward before tapering off toward the top. The deck housed the largest section of view screens, which wrapped around the front of the command deck. Command also accounted for the bulk of backup systems within the whole ship. Boosting command's front-row seats toward the action was both aesthetically pleasing and visually important. Practically though, constructing such a visible weakness at the heart of command was arrogant. You wouldn't see that type of construction on a Jumjul vessel.

I stalked through the corridors, fury pushing me forward. The majority of doors had labels for conference rooms or offices.

Popular jute stores peddled adventure stories of past and imagined future crews, citing thrilling escapades and heartwarming love stories. The reality was far from it. Command ran the whole outfit. Do you really think they were the ones who risked it all, venturing out into the unknown with the ever-present risk of death? Nope. Those missions were reserved for personnel who were top in their respective classes but ultimately expendable.

Sure, command got to make all the momentous decisions, but the record keeping at the end of the day was just as lousy as the swamp the *Rapscallion* was slowly sinking into.

The tourist placards indicated we were a few turns away from the main bridge. Good, I was ready for Mrs. Gol.

Cain sped up and moved to stop me.

"Get out of my way."

"We need a plan."

"Doors open, and bye-bye, one Mrs. Gol."

"That's not a plan."

"What, cause you're not the star of the whole show? Can't claim some heroic deed to move you up in the ranks?" When I'm angry, my brain has a way of spewing vitriol.

Cain snarled. "Keeping you alive is enough."

"Then what's the problem?"

"I thought you wanted answers."

"I do," I snapped. I did. He was right, and I didn't want to hear it. All I wanted to do was wipe that sanctimonious smile off Mrs. Gol's face—permanently.

"Don't you think she knows she's got you wound up

tighter than a reactor coil? She wants you off-balance," Cain said.

"Who cares?" I stepped to one side and tried to shove past him.

Cain didn't budge. In what might have been childish or a good tactical move, I moved again, that time aiming for his tail with one decisive stomp. When I planted my right foot firmly on top of it, Cain yelped. Then he roared.

"Get out of my way," I said, trying to ignore the look of death he threw me.

"If you die, I have nothing."

"Oh, how sad. The big IGJ man won't make rank. Boohoo."

"You're impossible," he growled.

"Good."

Unfortunately, Cain's little scene had stopped me long enough to clear my head somewhat. Even more upsetting was how right he was. I worked hard not to broadcast that thought, but by the glimmer in his eyes, he knew I'd already conceded.

"Fine. What's your brilliant plan?"

"Activate the door and let me go in first. My reflexes are sharper than yours"—he held up a hand to silence my reply, at least my verbal one—"and give you time to find cover."

I followed his line of thinking. "There'll be security on the bridge, but hiding behind a workstation or console would make it harder for their targeting systems. Provided their designs allow for that."

"They do."

"Really?" I crossed my arms and raised an eyebrow.

"Pulled up the schematics."

I rolled my eyes. Would've been useful to know a lot earlier that he could do that. "I swear you're making this harder than it should be at times."

"I don't trust you."

That simple statement hit me square in the chest. I got the fact he would've been suspicious of my involvement with Jorge's murder at first, but somewhere along the way, I'd assumed he'd moved past that. I was wrong and clearly needed to move back to not trusting him either.

Without another word, I moved up to the door and waited. Cain moved to my side, his body tight with anticipation. After only a few seconds, the double doors slid open, revealing the heart of the *Rapscallion*.

Cain pushed past me, his weapon lighting up the area directly in front of us. I rushed forward, noted a console to my left, and ducked down under its overhang. Despite an explosion of weapons fire, I chanced a quick peek around the base of the console and pulled back as a shot ricocheted off Cain's shielding.

After a quick glance around the area, I felt frustrated at not finding anything that might help even the odds. Personal shielding was an enormous advantage but wasn't designed for sustaining long periods of fire. The shield generators needed time to replenish. The whole add-on had been designed with duck-and-cover maneuvers in mind.

As I scanned the area again, my gaze got snagged on Confore's logo, stamped to the underside of the console. I scowled. Evading a corporation with tendrils in everything was going to be difficult. Maybe that was something my lawyers would be able to address, to find a loophole to protect me.

The space was as grand as the concept of the *Rapscallion*: numerous stations for officers and crew alike, along with a raised dais in the middle for the captain to keep her fingers on the pulse of the ship. The design was impressive but deadly for someone like me. All of that room and all those different workstations meant numerous places for Mrs. Gol to hide.

"Welcome, dear. You certainly know how to make an old woman wait, don't you?"

From my vantage point, I could hear her voice but not see her. I slid the XS-52 forward, ready to fire if need be.

"Cain?"

"His tour has come to an end."

Dread filled my heart, and my emotions flip-flopped. Cain was frustrating, annoying, and a whole host of things I didn't understand. Despite the apparent mistrust, he was still an ally in the whole messed-up situation. He was a reluctant ally, one I wasn't sure was welcome, but at least having him had been something. Because I'd had very little to start with, losing even a fraction of what I did have was devastating.

"There's no need to hide. If I wanted to kill you, I would have done so by now. Come on out, dear."

I gritted my teeth.

It was now or never.

Rising, I turned and trained my weapon on the smiling face of one very annoying lady, who, of course—cue eye roll—was seated in the captain's chair. I should've seen that one coming.

Cain lay on his side, with a growing pool of blood coating the floor. Keeping the XS-52 trained on Mrs. Gol, I knelt down to check his pulse. It was there, faint but still there.

"He needs medical treatment."

"Does he? It's no matter. The autosanitation bots will take care of the mess."

I fired the XS-52 just off to the side of the captain's chair. That earned me a wide-eyed look and then an admonishment.

"That's no way to act, child. Surely, your father taught you some manners, after all, didn't he?"

"Cain needs medical attention."

A cloud of annoyance passed over Mrs. Gol's face, and I fired again.

"Either treat him, or we end this."

"Silly girl. Do you think I went to all this trouble to get you here and let you shoot me?"

Okay, so I'm sure you're asking yourself why I didn't shoot the sanctimonious piece of space junk and be done with it. Cain was bleeding out, and I had a clear line of sight. One well-aimed shot, and the nightmare would be over. I would be free to help Cain and get off that doomed ship.

Believe me, I asked myself the same questions—yelled a few of them, actually. But remember that pesky little bug of curiosity? As much as I wanted to be done with everything, I was finally there in command, where she'd wanted me to go all along. The curiosity won out. Yes,

I'm well aware of the Old Earth saying, "Curiosity killed the cat." But I'm not the one with a tail. Whoops. Sorry, that was a bit insensitive.

Either way, her words were an open challenge. So I aimed for the chair's pedestal and fired. I should've guessed that command-level personnel would have layers of protection. The fire was absorbed by a force field. Cain hadn't stood a chance of doing anything but providing a heroic death to this whole charade.

I had nothing to bargain with except my life. But she would know that for the biggest bluff in bluff history.

I stood and looked down at Cain. All I could do was hope one of his IGJ bioupgrades included some kind of biobuilder tech, temporary nanobots that could diagnose and seal off a wound if triggered. That was Glipglow tech. I didn't know too much about how the system worked, only hoped that it did if he had it.

Please don't die. When his tail twitched ever so slightly, I almost slipped up with a huge grin of relief.

I forced the grin back and instead turned my full attention to Mrs. Gol. "All right. So I'm here. What's the big deal, anyway?"

For once, the old woman remained silent, simply staring at me.

"Um, hello? Mrs. Gol?"

She blinked. "Do you have any idea how much work it takes to discover the corporation behind the corporations that run this little tour outfit?" When I didn't answer, she sighed. "Years, my dear. And after that was accomplished, it took quite a bit more work to grease the right wheels to become a board member. The easiest bit of all was gaining enough credits to be able to direct my pet project how I saw fit." Her fingers stroked the arms of the captain's chair. "Quite a feat but well worth the time and expense. I knew you'd enjoy the latest addition to the tour. It's been an excellent investment."

"I wouldn't call commercializing torture and misery a good investment," I snapped.

"All in the eyes of the beholder, I suppose," Mrs. Gol shook her head slightly and abruptly changed topics. "How much do you know of the *Rapscallion*?"

"I'm not in the mood for another of your tour guide impressions."

"That's rather a rude stance. Just answer the question, please."

I sucked in a deep breath to smother my frustration. If I wanted answers, I would have to play along—not my cup of tea, but fine.

Regurgitating what I knew, along with a few points she'd made when we began the tour, Mrs. Gol listened and nodded when I finished.

"Standard information, I see. I would've thought you'd be able to do better."

My temper flared. "Better? What do you want from me, lady? I've played along, I watched the little horror show about my pops, and now I'm here, waiting for you to tell me what this has all been about while Cain bleeds out in front of us."

Mrs. Gol slid out of the chair, and defensively, I raised my weapon. Maybe I wasn't in the mood for answers after all. But she raised a finger and actually wagged it at me.

"Don't be naive."

"Tell me what you want, for Jupiter's sake."

"I want you to know the truth. To fully comprehend what your father did, how he crippled humanity with his betrayal."

"We won, if you haven't been keeping up," I snapped.

"Oh, we might have won in the sense of defeating the Eeri and driving them back to where they belong. But what we lost in the process was far greater than what anyone ever realized."

In a blatant show of confidence, Mrs. Gol turned her back to me and walked to the edge of the dais, presumably staring at the blank view screens. "The schematics of the ship. It's evident you have some working knowledge of this. Yet there is one area you don't know about. Very few do, more's the pity."

I was ready to throw another insult her way, but she looked up.

"Have you ever truly considered what might be above us?"

"Standard classified intel. All ships and records have their secrets."

As the words left my mouth, things clicked into place. One part of the *Rapscallion*, no one had ever been able to report on. Standard military statements glossed over questions concerning what else the *Rapscallion* might've housed. Why had this ship needed so many classified decks above command? Everyone knew the military was always seeking to improve weapons, ship AI cores, and their prowess within the larger galactic community. In time, though, reporters and watchdog groups either uncovered the truth of clandestine military programs or forced the government to fess up. That hadn't been true this time.

Whatever was above us had been zipped up tighter than an airlock's seals.

I suppose we'd grown accustomed to the fact that people in power—military, government, corporations, and the like—lied to the masses. Inundated with reminders about those lies, the populace had grown conditioned to shrug at the lies and continue with business. Early on, I'd been curious to know what was up there, but when I had been unable to get anywhere with the mountains of redacted reports, I turned my attention elsewhere.

My brief stint with a therapist hadn't gone well, nor had it been eye-opening. The woman had stated I was in denial and proceeded to tell me what a horrible human my pops was.

I knew I was in denial. How could I not be, trying to reconcile my memories of Pops, who was loving, caring, and always there for us even if we didn't like the lessons he tried to teach? How could I put those memories up against a man charged with aiding our enemy? Of being the cause of so many deaths?

If you can figure that out, then by all means, I'll listen. My denial helped me believe Pops had some kind of grand, overarching philosophy allowing him to do what he did. He must have had an ethical or moral stance he just couldn't ignore and, despite popular theory and opinion, had believed he was doing the right thing in aiding the Eeri.

He'd always stood up for what he believed, no matter

how unpopular the cause was. Nor did he care whom he stood up for. He was always ready to help someone in need, no matter their rank, station in life, or species. I'd let myself believe that his latest project for helping someone had been the Eeri.

I turned my wandering thoughts back to Mrs. Gol's question.

"But it's not like they'd leave anything up there with tourists wandering around."

"A correct assumption, for the most part. The more sensitive technology was stripped right after the *Rapscallion* crashed on Quarter's Landing. Questions would be raised, no doubt, for anyone who managed to access the deck. But without understanding the gravity of what was to be accomplished or whom to turn to with those questions, inquiring minds wouldn't get too far. That was seen to.

"But you know, don't you?" Mrs. Gol asked as she turned, her face almost unrecognizable. Tears glistened on her cheeks, her skin ashen. Gone was the chipper old woman who'd befriended me, drugged me, and led me on a merry chase. "Come with me."

I glanced down at Cain, relieved to see the pool of blood hadn't grown. *<Still with me?>* His tail moved just enough to provide confirmation. *<Good. Don't die.>*

16

This Stuff Keeps Getting Weirder and Weirder

Mrs. Gol stepped down from the captain's dais and wove through the consoles and workstations to the far side of the bridge. As she stood there and stared at the wall, I wondered if maybe she'd finally lost her last marbles. Then she lifted her right hand and placed her palm against the smooth metal wall. I almost cracked a joke and asked her if she needed a moment alone with the ship, but before I said anything unwise, a panel roughly double the size of her hand popped open. That was unexpected. From my vantage point, the compartment appeared to be a hidden control pad backlit with ominous red lighting.

"You were a part of the crew?" I asked.

She twisted to look at me and waved her hand. "No. At least, not all of me was."

"Excuse me?"

Before Mrs. Gol decided to answer, she shifted her body to obscure the series of codes she entered to trigger a facial and retinal scan. After she passed those security measures, the panel's lights switched from red to green. Off to Mrs. Gol's left, pressurized air hissed out through a seam running up the wall, back toward Mrs. Gol, and down to the floor.

"Turns out money can buy anything." She lifted a hand and twisted the appendage back and forth. "This came from Lieutenant Commander Ives, a woman of excellent lineage and stationed on Cloud-11 after her tour onboard the *Rapscallion*."

"Please tell me she checked the little donor box on her bioreadout and you suffered a tragic accident that resulted in the loss of your hand."

"Would that make you feel better?"

I gaped at her. *Did she really ask that?* I thought. I mean, come on.

"Such limited thinking."

"Limited thinking? What did you do, invite the woman over for tea and casually ask for her hand—her literal hand—so you could access a secret panel on a former military ship? Just nonchalantly throwing in there how she won't miss such a vital part of her body, I'm sure."

"In essence, it was Commander Ives's idea. Also Commander Tuk and the captain's."

My stomach rolled as I connected the dots. This wasn't some fun little time-wasting kids' activity, which revealed a prancing unicorn or big fluffy puppy. Flesh and horror completed this connect-the-dots game. The keypad's security measures must have included fingerprint scanners, and if I understood what the deranged woman was inferring, the retinal scan upset me even further. The truly nauseating part of her little revelation was the facial recognition scan.

What Mrs. Gol had revealed meant I'd been staring at, talking to, and smiling at a dead person's face for the past couple of days. I would have to reconsider my stance on therapists if I survived.

"I know what you think, dear. Yes, the procedures were quite an arduous process—to sculpt my face in such a way as to ensure the ship's security measures recognized my new facial features, yet not enough to trip off any alarms with general security protocols. As I said, money can buy you anything."

"Did they at least do this all willingly?" I hated to but felt compelled to ask.

"In the end, yes, when they realized the stakes, the magnitude of it all. I so greatly appreciate their brave sacrifices."

I narrowed my eyes. I didn't think Mrs. Gol understood the question, but I'd gotten my answer.

"Now, it's time for you to learn the truth of what happened during the Cricade Wars."

"If that involves surrendering bits and pieces of me, you can count me out."

Mrs. Gol laughed as I cringed. "Don't be silly. Come along."

If I was ever going to recognize what walking into the land of lunatic crazy looked like, that was my opportunity. At least I could boast I'd gotten the full tour of the ship.

I glanced over my shoulder at Cain and was relieved

to find him staring right back and conscious. He was an annoying, uptight, handsome specimen of a man, irritating and extremely annoying... I said that already, didn't I? Anyway, I felt reassured to see he should live through the whole mess.

My finger hovered over the XS-52's trigger, itching to fire as I ducked into the creepy, hidden corridor after Mrs. Gol. A few well-placed shots might not take her down, but I had no idea what nightmare-fueled creepy-crawly things might lurk in a ship stuck in a swamp, with no one monitoring the area.

To my surprise and relief, lights flared to life above us as we made our way through the narrow corridor. The space was at least half the size of the other passageways throughout the ship. We passed exposed panels, wiring, and conduits. That area definitely wasn't up to code. I paused to look at one of the open panels and realized the conduits had been ripped out. The jagged edges along the connectors, at both ends, weren't typical of damage incurred during an attack. That was a rush job done with brute strength.

The corridor was designed with a gentle upward slope, and after a few minutes, the walkway opened and expanded into a cavernous area, the perfect place for a sneak attack—like in some Old Earth movies where you know no one in their right mind would go, but they do. You watch the show, yell at the characters, and throw popcorn at the screen, believing somehow that doing so will get them to turn around and ignore the creepy old house. But the characters never do, do they?

"I admit I'm disappointed in how little you understand

of the *Rapscallion* and your father's actions. I had been operating under the assumption he trained you."

I frowned. "Trained me? Pops was a xenologist."

"Ah, yes. My apologies."

Mrs. Gol stepped into the darkness and drew in a deep breath, her shoulders arched up toward her head, and as a new set of lights came to life, she exhaled long and slow.

I lifted the arm with the XS-52, ready for someone or something to leap out at me, but as my eyes adjusted to the new light, one glance around the room revealed the people weren't going to do anything but haunt my dreams.

The space encompassed the entire top part of the *Rapscallion*. No decks were above us, no other hidden rooms, just one enormous open-concept workspace.

Or whatever the space had been designed for.

Along the edges of the room were dozens upon dozens of workstations and screens, all sitting in the dark and patiently waiting for someone to clock in and go to work. What the work had been, I didn't have the foggiest. Whom that work had been for, I could hazard a guess.

A few meters or so from the row of what I presumed were the main workstations, another row of stations sat. Smaller pedestal consoles butted up against their own medical platforms. Even from my vantage point at the entrance, I could see the majority of the beds were still occupied by desiccated skeletons of humanoid configuration.

The scene reminded me of the work Pops had overseen on Est-E 24, a world abandoned by a colony lost to the ripples of history. The job was one of a handful he'd done for the IGJ when the IGJ commissioned a group of forensic scientists, archaeologists, and recovery specialists to work there. Pops's meticulous work record landed him the job of coordinating the entire thing. The IGJ had decided the time had come to unravel the mystery of Est-E 24 and figure out what had happened to a once-thriving colony.

Pops allowed my brother and me to do as we pleased for the majority of our time on Est-E 24. I was probably no more than fifteen or so. We hadn't been on world long before I grew bored and wandered over to where Pops worked. They'd uncovered over a hundred dead colonists. Their bodies exhumed from their unintentional graves, all were laid out with compassion on medical platforms for identification and examination of any clues to what had happened to them.

Those remains had been handled with dignity and respect, while these had been left to rot. Who in their right mind walked by so many dead while they ripped out tech but ignored the human bodies? Not someone I would ever want to meet. But despite the horror of so many dead, forgotten, and entombed in the darkness, the center of the room demanded my attention.

A thick tube constructed out of a transparent material, large enough to need six or seven of me to encircle the object, was the centerpiece. Its base was secured into the flooring while the top extended a few meters upward, just shy of the ceiling. Pale-blue lights glowed along the base, pulsating sequentially in intensity, round and round, like some kind of ominous countdown sequence.

Inside the tube was the only body in the room left with flesh. The body's skin carried a sallow tint, the man suspended by an intricate maze of thin metallic tubing.

Mrs. Gol walked over to the tube and placed a hand against it. "Hello, Triton. I've missed you."

For a moment, I expected another set of controls to appear, but then I saw the look she was casting over the poor soul inside the tube. She was mourning.

"Who's Triton?" Even though she might've been a crazy, unstable woman, I could still show an ounce of sympathy.

A long, heavy silence passed between us before she answered.

"My son."

17

Who Was
Wats Hawking Orion?

Bizarre thoughts ran through my mind as I tried desperately to understand what Mrs. Gol wanted from me until they stopped on one word: "retribution." Or at least some form of revenge. For a few, brief moments, I suspended my own sanity and reluctantly admitted she didn't seem quite so crazy.

I won't lie—I've had my fair share of dreams detailing how I would've rescued Pops. The majority of scenarios featured me, guns blazing, as I ripped through the *Rapscallion* and its crew to emerge victorious with Pops safely in tow. In others, I hired a team of retcon mercs, all loyal to me and bent on making sure Pops was retrieved without a scratch. Those are the desperate dreams of a daughter who loved her pops, who was clinging to the hope that his misdeeds were false or at least for some noble reason no one could admit because, for some inexplicable reason, the ones in power had needed a scapegoat.

In the deep darkness of the long nights, those thoughts and dreams drifted into the part of me I was afraid to acknowledge. When I got lost in those thoughts, I was frightened by the certainty of knowing I could inflict pain on those who'd hurt Pops.

Could I find a difference between the part of me I'd buried deep inside and someone like Mrs. Gol? I couldn't miss the love and adoration etched upon her face as she gazed on the lifeless body of her son. That love was no different from what I felt for Pops. Mrs. Gol and I had both suffered immense losses yet ended up on very different paths in creating a way forward through our grief and pain. Perhaps the only difference was Mrs. Gol hadn't truly found a way forward. She'd walked back toward her son, while I had learned to walk away. Or at least, I had tried to.

"Was he an officer?"

Mrs. Gol shook her head as her hand slid off the container. "No. He was so much more than that."

She turned to face me, the facade of a pleasant older woman gone. In its place was her true visage. She saw the world through eyes clouded by hate and a thirst for retribution.

"Whatever happened here, I wasn't a part of it." I stepped back, hands held out by my sides.

"Not directly. No. But someone must pay. Someone must understand what was taken from us."

"When you say, 'from us,' can you clarify?" I asked, trying to get a straight answer. I sidestepped to my right, putting one of the medical platforms between Mrs. Gol and myself. While the woman wasn't carrying an obvious weapon, the word "obvious" no longer meant much. If she finally had her fill of her game, at least the medical platform would provide some kind of cover.

"From humanity. From what we are promised."

Great, more riddles. I wished she would say what she meant instead of beating around the proverbial bush.

"You'll have to give me more than that. I'm afraid I don't subscribe to the Future Forecasts Weekly."

A sneer coated her face and twisted her features into a monstrous visage. "My son was born and bred for this. They all were—generations handpicked for what was to come, raised amongst the finest families, educated by the brightest minds. And for what? For one man to turn the tide against them. To betray his own people."

My head began to hurt as confusion heaped itself upon stinking piles of confusion. A dull throb took up residence at the base of my neck. I was running on empty. I needed a good night's sleep and time to sort through the whole mess. "I don't understand. What are you talking about?"

"For generations, we've known what was coming. Those lucky enough to be visited by the visions began to prepare, to pave the way for those who would usher in a new era, a dawning of the glorious ascension of humankind."

"Have you been hanging out with the Star Eaters or something? I swear, you people and your cryptic messages. Cut to the chase, lady."

Mrs. Gol's eyes burned. "You hear but don't listen. You see but are blind. Your father knew of what was to come. He was one of us. Wats Hawking Orion—he was the best of us until he polluted the gene pool with you and your fiend of a brother."

Any advice on how to handle the news that your pops, a man you'd defended, believed in when the entire universe stood against him, might have been a part of something so crazy, so far-fetched it had to be true? I wasn't completely ready to take that madwoman at face value, but I'd seen enough to know much more was going on than I could ever have imagined.

The dull throb constricted into a knot and worked its way up the back of my skull. I reached up and tried to massage the area but only succeeded in creating a fresh wave of pain. I squeezed my eyes shut to clear the momentary blur of vision.

<Mahia.>

My eyes snapped open. That was no headache or whispered memory. I knew that voice.

"Are you ready to face the truth of how and what your father did? How he managed to destroy the future of humanity?" She added in a smaller voice, "How he murdered my son?"

I blinked a few more times and twisted my neck back and forth to try to relieve some of the building tension. "Sure, go ahead," I croaked.

"Then see with eyes of clarity. Hear with ears unclouded."

A bit dramatic, but okay.

"What the—"

Smoke billowed up from the floor, and the room was bathed in soft green hues. I crouched, the XS-52 geared up and ready, and tried to clear my head of the flashbacks from my one and only rave. That's a story for a time when I'm not trying to unravel the mysteries of the universe.

Whispers rolled through the smoke. Bits and pieces of conversation swirled in the surrounding air. Those whispers grew stronger and morphed into a dozen different conversations at once. Shadows moved through the haze, and I tucked myself underneath the medical platform. My heart matched the pounding in my head as a pair of pleated trousers moved past me.

What in Jupiter's name had just happened?

<Holograms.>

The word exploded inside my skull, and I grabbed my head and whimpered from the pain. <*This is not the time to experiment with extra-sensory abilities,*> I grumbled.

<*It is.*>

<*Well, you'd better stop, or I'm going to pass out.*>

Merciful rings of Saturn, he did. Who would've guessed his telepathy wasn't a one-way street? If it wasn't wreaking so much havoc with my head, I would've mentally high-fived him.

As Cain's presence receded, though I could still feel the crafty bugger, I focused on the medical platform's support. Long rectangular tubes were coated a drab gray and bolted to the floor. My fingers brushed its cool metallic surface, and I took deep, even breaths. My vision gradually cleared.

Holograms made sense, I ruefully admitted. The whole projection system had been a part of her plan, to reveal how adept Mrs. Gol had become in commandeering the *Rapscallion*'s systems. She'd all but admitted being behind the whole installation, which meant she'd had the opportunity to add whatever programming or software she'd wanted.

With that simply marvelous understanding of the situation, I pulled myself up and noted how the smoke was settling along the floor. With a grunt and a fresh wave of dizziness, I grabbed hold of the platform to steady myself.

Mrs. Gol continued to stand by her son, her eyes dull as the scene she'd orchestrated unfurled around us.

It was an opportune time to strike or at least turn and run.

You guessed it. I did neither.

Instead, I stood there like a fool. Want to know why?

Because the hologram in front of me was none other than Pops.

That was the image of Pops I remembered, a strong man, just a few inches shy of six feet, his body lean and sturdy from years of moving through unstable terrain and manual labor. Dressed in a jumpsuit, he stood on the opposite side of the medical platform, examining a hologram of a young woman superimposed over her skeletal remains.

"Pulse dropping, blood pressure isn't holding steady. Neural activity is fading." Another man, a little shorter than Pops and dressed in the regalia of command, looked up from the medical platform's console. "This'll make the fourth one today. And the seventh overall."

Pops clenched his jaw and furrowed his brow, all

classic signs of the man trying to work out a puzzle in his head. "Inadequate integration? Biorejections?"

The officer shook his head. "Tang, report."

A young woman dressed in the drab gray of medical scooted over from another console and handed Pops a data pad. He scrolled through the information, lips compressed in frustration.

"Doesn't make sense, does it? Everything checks out," Pops said.

"Except for one small, almost undetectable bacterium, something we would never have thought to look for if we hadn't salvaged those dead Eeri," the officer replied.

Anyone not familiar with Pops would more than likely have missed the slight tightening of his hands around the data pad. And the forceful swallow.

"Sabotage?" he asked, turning toward the officer.

"Of the highest magnitude." The man snapped his fingers, and security officers moved out from behind the tube, coming to stand on either side of Pops.

"Why?"

"You know why. None of this is what we thought."

The officer scowled. "You introduced that bacteria into the entire system. And now it's crawling around in our children, destroying generations of work and sacrifice."

The only answer Pops gave was to stand tall and stare at the officer.

"Take him," the man snapped.

The two security guards lifted their weapons, and

Pops left with them. He didn't resist or try to deny anything.

I closed my eyes against the feelings of betrayal. *Who were you?*

That was a new question to haunt my dreams. My faith in Pops had been unwavering through everything. Until right then, that moment. I sensed a seed of doubt taking hold inside my thoughts, ready to sprout and weave its vicious thorns through everything I thought I'd known.

"Damage report."

I opened my eyes at the new voice. A woman's voice was low and full of barely contained anger: Captain Tow.

"Ma'am, we've identified the bacteria but are currently unable to stop the spread. Nothing we've thrown at it is working. In fact, whatever we do only fuels the bacteria's growth."

"Nothing from Orion?"

"No, ma'am. Not yet."

Captain Tow scowled. "Damn him."

The captain turned to look at the young woman on the medical platform. "He'll pay for this." She reached down and smoothed the unresponsive woman's hair. "All these lives, lost. Years of research, of preparation, gone." Her hand lingered for a moment too long, then she snatched it away. But it was enough to reveal the depth of emotions a captain learned to bottle up inside.

"Triton?"

"We forced a shutdown. The bacteria are contained within the outer shielding. But we won't be able to try again until we can figure out how to neutralize the bacteria's effects."

The mask was back on Captain Tow's face. "Inform the families and the emperor." Her gaze gave the place one last sweep. "Shut it down. Shut it all down."

18

No More Coincidences

In a blink of an eye, the holograms disappeared. The room returned to its somber duty of standing guard over its dead, the men and women Pops had murdered. He was a person I no longer recognized, a man capable of standing next to all these people, watching them suffer, and not batting an eye.

"Now do you see?"

"See what?" I spat the words at her and blinked back tears. "A set of lies, fabricated by your insane beliefs?" I didn't want to believe anything I'd witnessed. How could I take any of it at face value, right? It was Mrs. Gol's theater, a program whose engineering she had overseen. Everything she had done was all some mixed-up, crazy delusion of a woman stuck in the abyss of grief.

Mrs. Gol shook her head, "You see but are still blind."

"I'm not the one who's blind!" I shouted at her and sucked in a deep breath. "My pops didn't do this. He couldn't have. He was a man of principle. I don't know what happened, but you're wrong. He couldn't… would never have murdered… He was set up or something."

"My poor child. What can I do to make you see? To open your mind to the truth?"

Mrs. Gol moved away from her son's unintentional tomb and walked to the nearest medical platform. "I knew your father well."

I snarled and raised my weapon. "Don't even think for a moment you can twist my memory of him into something hideous to suit your delusions." Protective shielding or not, I didn't care. I fired, raw, untamed emotions coursing through my body. All my shots ricocheted off her barrier and left scorch marks throughout the room.

My anger and futile attempts only made her stand there and cackle in delight. "Perhaps I'm getting through to you after all."

<Don't let her goad you.>

I pushed back against Cain's words. What did he care? The fight wasn't his. He only needed me to stay alive to boost his service record.

Mrs. Gol looked down at the skeleton, its lifeless eyes staring back up. With reverence, she brushed off the layers of dust covering its skull and cleared its eye sockets until the shroud of decay vanished.

"Your father had a tattoo, the image of a sun, on his left shoulder blade. Correct?"

Any thread of hope I was clinging to, wanting to believe everything was wild conjecture dreamed up for the papers of a jute-store novel, vanished with those words.

"Nothing ostentatious. An iconic representation of a sun." Mrs. Gol shrugged off her jacket. "Come here, child."

My heart screamed at my brain as my feet shuffled me over to her side. I didn't want to know, but I had to. My fingers trembled as I reached out and pulled back her blouse. There on her left shoulder was the faded but identifiable tattoo of a sun. My hand jerked back as if burned.

"Did he ever tell you why he chose that particular image to be forever seared upon his flesh?" Mrs. Gol calmly asked as she slipped her jacket back on.

All I could do was shake my head.

"My apologies, then." Mrs. Gol buttoned up her jacket. "I'm under the impression you don't carry the same mark."

I shook my head once more.

One day, a year or so before Pops left us, we'd finished up on Hiker's Marvel, less commonly known as Isoth. At one time, it'd been a place of unbridled technological development and artistic flourish. But time had worn its inhabitants down into nothing more than pale shadows of their former glory, and they were earning a living through the tourist trade. The wildlands and mountain ranges nearby were places for the outdoor adventurer to go.

What remained of the world's original inhabitants marked their bodies with the symbols of their ancient past, one last connection to remind them of what they'd once been.

I'd latched onto the idea and decided to get the same

tattoo Pops sported, a way to carry on a family tradition for which my wild-eyed youth had invented numerous tales. None of them were true, yet Pops always laughed and encouraged them. But when I told him I wanted the sun on my left shoulder, he abruptly turned cold and distant and told me, in no uncertain terms, I was to never mark my body. His tattoo was a mistake, one he deeply regretted.

In true Mahia fashion, I sneaked off later that night, finding my way to the less reputable trade areas. As I settled into the chair and awaited my turn, Pops showed up. That was one of the few times I saw his temper. His face, full of fury, scared the living daylights out of me, and I'd never entertained the idea of a tattoo again.

I found my voice as the question needed to be asked. "What does it mean?"

"For the uninitiated, nothing. It's simply a picture of the sun."

You would think she would fill me in at some point on what had happened, what was going on. But nope. In true villain fashion, Mrs. Gol turned her back and returned to stand at her son's side.

"It's all a lopsided coincidence. So what if you have the same tattoo. Maybe the image was popular at one time. Maybe there are a dozen or more who have the same thing. The odds would be in favor of it, especially if the idea had been pushed by some popular net-star or advertising company," I stubbornly reasoned.

"Wats Hawking Orion took the life of my son."

Oh, goodie, so we're jumping ahead to that part now, eh?

"It is only fitting I take a life of his own," Mrs. Gol solemnly stated.

"Hold up." I took a step back, realizing I really shouldn't have been suckered into getting closer to her. "That hologram display you so generously provided… It said the bacteria or whatever didn't make it all the way to Triton. So technically, Pops didn't kill him."

Mrs. Gol snarled. "Of course he did. Because of your father, the entire program was shut down." Her eyes blazed with anger. "They tried. Several times, they tried to flush the bacteria out of the system, to salvage what they could. Nothing worked. And in the end, everything was abandoned. No amount of pleas or credits could convince them otherwise. And so my son was forced to remain aboard this vessel, left to die as the living stripped this ship and its secrets abandoned."

Well, I'd tried. "So far, you've only shown me possibilities of what my Pops did, nothing conclusive. Why should I believe you? Why should I take any of this seriously?"

The answer came not from Mrs. Gol but rather from Cain, along with another stellar headache.

<She is telling the truth.>

<Be quiet,> I snapped. *<What could you possibly know?>*

<That she's telling the truth.>

<Well, isn't that convenient. You aren't even here. You're just eavesdropping where you aren't welcome.>

<Don't turn around.>

Well, blow me out an airlock and color me purple.

<Is there any way we can do this without the searing mind crunch?>

<It… should lessen in time.>

Should. Not a word of confidence. *<Great.>*

I turned my attention back to Mrs. Gol. "So, this has all been tit-for-tat, I take it."

"That's a rather crude way to put it, but yes."

"And how do you plan on killing me? If it involves something horribly painful, a few moments to prep would be great. It's been a pretty crummy day so far."

She shrugged. "You've had plenty of time to prepare."

I stared at her. She stared at me. My brain wanted to make several connections, but something was missing.

"What's that supposed to mean?"

Her focus shifted to her son. "I told you I would never leave you, and I've kept my promise."

Okay, so we're shifting into a whole other level of crazy now. "What's he say? Is he down with his mama's plan?"

"How dare you?" Mrs. Gol's eyes snapped back to mine. "You're not even worthy to stand in his presence, and yet you mock him? Mock me?"

Whatever bit of sanity was left in the old woman broke. She turned and full-on cooed at her dead son. She reached out and stroked the tube. Everything was a tad bit too creepy for my taste.

I gave her credit for having held on to her sanity as long as she had. The whole ordeal had been years in the making, not to mention the amount of credits the extensive planning had taken and all the work to get the holograms up and running, especially building that whole fun little scenario for me.

I chuckled inwardly. I would've hated to be the person on that help desk hotline.

Oh, for Jupiter's sake.

<Cain, how strong are you? Can you go back to the captain's chair?>

After a few unintelligible words, just impressions of annoyance, he sent, *<Yes.>*

<Good. Do it. I'll keep her distracted until you get there. Hurry.>

"So tell me, how could a mother let her child be put into"—I waved a nonchalant hand at the tube—"that thing?"

Too light an insult. She ignored me.

Take two. "I can't imagine what sort of uncaring, decrepit mother would allow her son to be strung up like a piece of garbage, something to be leered at by those who worked in here."

"You insolent child, you've no idea of what you speak."

I shrugged. "Well, I've watched my share of true-crime dramas, and let me tell you, it takes a pretty rotten individual to offer their offspring up to some kind of torture chamber like this one. I bet the ratings on a show that documented all this would be the highest ever. Maybe I should look at selling my pops's story. After all, you say it's all true, right?"

Perhaps I'd gone a little too far. Mrs. Gol launched herself at me. Whatever bioupgrades she'd sprung for must have included some nifty military ones, 'cause no way could a normal little old lady have leaped through the air over a medical platform to knock me flat on my back.

We spun away from each other, and as I looked up to assess the situation, she was already on her feet and moving in for the attack. I rolled off to the side and narrowly missed a vicious kick. Luck tossed me a bone, giving me time to scramble to my feet and put a medical platform between us.

<You were supposed to keep her talking, not attacking.>

"I know," I huffed in frustration.

"How dare you. I love my son. He was everything to me. Everything I did, every sacrifice, was for him."

"Do you think he would see it that way?" I asked as Mrs. Gol rushed around the corner of the platform.

"Of course. They all did, even your father, until he was corrupted by the piece of trash he called a wife."

Oh… oh no. My mom was a no-go area. I didn't know much about her, only that she'd died giving birth to my brother. Pops hardly ever talked about her, but when he did, it was always with that wistful look of love. I kept a few images of her, from when she and Pops had met, and I had visited her part of the family a few times before everything blew up around Pops. They were a nice lot, just not willing to forgive Pops for dragging her off into the wilds of the universe.

I raised the XS-52 and fired, straight and true at Mrs. Gol's chest. Her personal shielding deflected the blast but couldn't mitigate the force of the close-proximity shot. She was thrown back, and her body slammed against the edge of the next platform.

For a moment, I thought her back was broken, but

she plopped to the floor, instantly moved to all fours, and pushed herself back up.

<I'm here.>

I turned and ran. Moving down through the maze of skeletons, I made my way farther into the chamber of nightmares.

<Tell me what you see.>

<Standard cushions, well-built chair. Control pads built into the console.> After a pause, he said what I'd hoped to hear. *<The Confore logo.>*

Bingo.

<Access the control port under the right arm of the chair.>

I might not be a good hacker or have any idea about how to work a derelict ship's systems, but I was a damn good support person. If someone had a problem with a piece of Confore tech, I would find the solution, which also meant I knew a hundred different ways to short out a system.

<Huh.>

<Top that, IGJ man,> I smugly thought as something rammed into me.

Mrs. Gol slammed me into a platform, and my forehead bounced off the unforgiving metal surface. The room tilted and began to spin. I reached out and tried to grab hold of something but succeeded only in toppling a pile of bones as we all clattered to the floor.

Mrs. Gol's cold fingers wrapped around my neck. "You're not going anywhere. You'll die here as my Triton did. And together, I'll keep watch over you both."

"I'm not really the marrying kind," I managed to gasp.

<What am I supposed to do with this?>

<Hold, please,> I thought in my best help desk voice. On the verge of passing out, I managed to get my arms up around Mrs. Gol's vise grip and went for her eyes. That was a scenario I'd hoped never to have to use, but it did the trick. I pressed my thumbs against the soft, squishy flesh, and within seconds, she let out a cry and tumbled off me.

<You should be looking at a 3.56 version of Confore's Revitalizing Memories holographic unit.>

<I am.>

Good thing the Weplies are fanatic labelers. *<Pull out the third data card and put it in the empty slot beneath the others.>*

I continued to throw Cain instructions as I picked up the nearest thing I could brandish as a weapon, a femur. *Forgive me*, I thought. Pops had instilled in me a respect for the dead. I hoped whoever owned those bones wouldn't be too upset. But again, they would've been on Mrs. Gol's side. Too bad.

She rushed at me again, and I landed a satisfying blow to the side of her face. Protective shielding was typically designed for weapons fire or long-range combat tactics. She'd been a fool not to buy the hand-to-hand-combat upgrade.

<Got it.>

<Replace the cover and switch it on.>

All I can say is thank goodness for people who never read instructions and think they can do things on their own. That was a common issue, probably in the top ten for Revitalizing Memories. Everyone thought the programming was based on standard interfaces with the main AI nodes and the data cards. But Confore had experimented and switched up their usual coding standards, trying to be all fancy with that model. Confore's plan had backfired, and they'd released Revitalizing Memories 4 with an apology discount. Just one week ago.

Every single hologram programmed into Mrs. Gol's little chamber of nightmares sprang to life. The unit boasted an impressive amount of memory and stored discarded images or various versions of the program. Praise be to the Weplies.

The room transformed from a somber tomb into the party of a lifetime. If the holograms had been solid, it would've been standing room only at this impromptu little shindig.

My hopes rested on how far Mrs. Gol had traveled into loony land. The cacophony of voices and the abrupt appearance of all those she had believed in, and presumably known, did the trick.

I spared Mrs. Gol a glance as she pushed herself up and looked around in confusion at the hustle and bustle around her. Officers moved from platform to platform, inspecting the damage. All the still bodies of those offered as sacrifices to who knows what appeared. As she struggled to get her bearings, I worked my way among the medical platforms and inadvertently walked through Pops.

My mind knew he was only another hologram, but that jarred me enough to stop me. I turned to look at his fabrication and questioned everything I thought I'd known. That image was different from the one Mrs. Gol had previously shown me. Pops was standing off to the side and watching. His hand reached up and touched the small pendant he'd always worn, the only thing my brother had ever stated he wanted before up and vanishing into the cosmos.

"It doesn't matter where you go or what you do. Everything has unfolded as your father planned!" Mrs. Gol screeched.

"Whatever," I muttered and got the heck out of there.

19

Unwanted Revelations

As I made my way back to the bridge, I spun around and fired at Mrs. Gol's hidden control panel. A series of satisfying crackles and pops accompanied the door clicking shut. The crazy lady wouldn't be getting out of that—at least, I hoped not.

"I take it whatever you instructed me to do, worked."

"Seems to." I turned to throw Cain a huge grin, but as I did, the room went sideways, and my legs turned to jelly.

Everything blurred as though I was looking through a window that desperately needed to be cleaned. A blob moved toward me, and I hoped to Jupiter it was Cain.

"What's wrong?"

I tried to wave him off. "Must be the aftereffects of whatever Mrs. Gol sedated me with." As I struggled to push myself into a sitting position, Cain's hands gripped my arms and helped me.

"A sedative shouldn't have this kind of effect," he said.

Medical stuff wasn't my forte. But what else could

it be? I'd been in tough situations before, scrapes that required a lot more physically than that little adventure. I wasn't some weak damsel in distress who needed someone to save her, even if that someone was as good-looking as Cain.

"The sedative might have interacted with some lingering effects of the poison," I guessed.

I mean, good grief, how much of all this nasty business with people wanting me dead could my body take? Not to mention that Mrs. Gol had also been kind enough to shoot me.

"Wait, how are you up and around? Last I saw, you were lying in a puddle of blood."

I felt his grimace even though I couldn't see it.

"Repair bots are doing what they can."

"Is that always the answer? Bioupgrades and the like fixing things?"

"An advantage of our times."

I snorted. "We make a fine pair then, huh?" I quipped. My body was losing steam, but my mind still worked away. "She must've laced the sedative with something else. Crazy lady wanted me dead, you know."

"If true, it only means we need to get you help."

I snorted. "Good luck with that. The *Starshine* left. The employees left."

"There are still a few emergency shuttles."

At least someone thought ahead, I thought with a hint of optimism. I'd been so bent on getting answers, which hadn't happened—thanks, universe—that I hadn't thought too much about the details of an exit strategy.

"Can't you signal the IGJ or something?" A shiver ran through my body.

"Too far out."

"Where's the nearest port?"

After a moment of silence, he answered. "Starbase 9.2. Medical services are limited there, but the odds would be better than staying here." He didn't let me throw in my two cents, not that my opinion would have mattered at that point, but instead shifted positions and slid his arms underneath mine to lift me.

I giggled, unable to stop myself.

He snarled.

The first few steps he took were wide and a little unsteady. He shifted my weight and proceeded, but the heroic gesture was obviously exacting its toll on him. Not having to expend any physical energy, I tried to concentrate on the small, annoying tickle at the back of my mind. "You're not trying to throw some thoughts or something my way, are you?"

"No."

All right, then, something else was bothering me. I wasn't prepared to dwell on the highly likely scenario that I had no idea who Pops had been. Those were rev-elations to tuck away for later, when everything settled down and I could face the problem logically, with a clear head. No, I was currently being annoyed by something Mrs. Gol had said.

I closed my eyes, the slight seesawing effect of being in Cain's arms making me slightly nauseous.

What was bothering me was the phrasing of what Mrs. Gol had said as I'd scooted away, something about how everything was unfolding as planned. No, that wasn't quite right. *"Unfolding as… it'd been planned"*? Nope. *"Unfolding as…"* Saturn's ill-begotten rings. *"Unfolding as your father planned."* That's how she'd said it.

Pops certainly hadn't planned for my death, to be trapped on a ship with a crazy old woman who relished dragging his name through the swampy nether lands. What he had planned, according to her, was the death of all those people. But… What? He'd introduced bacteria into the system.

"You'll die here, just as my Triton did." That nifty little phrase popped up in my head too. I'd assumed she'd just been speaking generally, as in she was going to kill me in the same place her son had died.

My poor, tired synapses made the connection. That piece of space junk had poisoned me with the same bacteria Pops had introduced into the system all those years ago. I would have been furious if not for an immediate rush of fear. If I was right, then I was dead. If Mrs. Gol's teatime groupies hadn't solved the problem before, with presumably the best and brightest at their disposal, who was going to save me now?

Cain's hands tightened their grip. "We're almost to the shuttles. Hold on."

My mouth went dry, and my tongue was heavy and sticky. I was too tired to even try to move my lips. But I wanted to tell him, to let him know.

<*I know.*>

The next few minutes or hours—I couldn't tell any longer—just floated past me. Cain took us to the shuttle bay and awkwardly tried to hold me as he fiddled with the controls to jack us a shuttle. He had a few tense words and worried expressions for me as he laid me in one of the shuttle's seats and strapped me in.

I wanted to ask if he'd had any pilot training or if we were both going on a grand new adventure.

The last thing I distinctly remember hearing Cain say was, "Huh."

20

TricLath Pudding, Part Two

"Get them off." Cain's growl, familiar by then, filled the room as my eyes fluttered open.

If not for his voice, I would've succumbed to the idea that I was once again stuck with Mrs. Gol on the *Rapscallion*. The whole business of getting drugged, passing out, and waking up someplace different was getting tiresome.

Someone's reply came with the sensation of something cold running across my forehead. "Stomp your feet to shake them loose."

Involuntarily, I tried to jerk away, but something strong and heavy closed around my head to keep me in place.

"Hold still," the second person said. "We must check to see if your body has flushed the last of the bacterium out."

I wasn't having any luck ascertaining who or what was talking. Squeezing my eyes closed and then blinking hard several times, I tried to clear my vision, but the world remained clouded.

"Our apologies. Here."

Something pulled against my skin, and all at once, everything sprang into clarity.

"A temporary shield and restorative energy field. Of our own design."

Hovering over me was none other than a Glipglow. If my recognition of the species individuality markers were correct, this was the same Glipglow who'd come to my aid on the *Starshine*.

My brow furrowed in confusion as I managed to push myself up. "How?"

The Glipglow's attention momentarily turned to Cain, who was spinning in a circle while trying to jump up and down.

I tried to smother my laugh at the sight of him. "Aw, they like you," I cooed.

Cain sent me a death glare and yipped when one of the little chompers nipped his hand as he tried to get the hatchling off the edge of his jacket.

"Get them off," he growled again.

I do believe the Glipglow paused a few moments too long before sucking in a lungful of air and letting off a series of vibrations. In an instant, the little ones released their hold and scattered.

Cain smoothed his affronted clothing and turned to face me. "You have Master of Dentar to thank."

I raised my eyebrows. A Master Glipglow? I sat up a little taller and bowed my head in thanks. Glipglows are renowned for their longevity, with lifespans easily quadruple the length, if not more, of a typical human's. The title of Master bestowed upon a Glipglow signified at least two hundred years of study in their chosen field, plus another fifty in a variety of supplementary subjects.

Once a Glipglow gained the title, the general understanding was that they would spend the rest of their lives in service to what roughly translates as the den mother in their capital city and would work with engineers and architects to use their vast wealth of knowledge in all sorts of advancements.

"You are fortunate our little hatchlings were due for their first excursion off world. We do not know of another who could solve your mystery."

Masters were also well known for their egos. But I would say if an individual spent all that time studying one subject, they deserved to flaunt their brilliance. I certainly wasn't going to sit there and argue.

"Thank you, Master of Dentar. I'm in your debt."

"We are in your debt," Cain added.

I threw him a look, but he refused to meet my gaze. Fine.

The pieces all fell down in front of me. "So. Mrs. Gol—" The gears in my brain locked in place. "Wait, what about Mrs. Gol?"

"The authorities were contacted. The *Rapscallion* has been quarantined. The likelihood of her survival until the IGJ arrives is slim to none. The ship finished its cycle and shut down."

I can't say I was sorry. If the ship shut down, the air recyclers were offline. Life support would be minimal at best to conserve energy and save the owners a few credits.

I picked up where I had taken an abrupt U-turn. "So,

Mrs. Gol poisoned me with the same junk that was used to kill—" I stopped myself before I let the truth slip out. "With some type of bioweapon onboard the *Rapscallion*. Was it in the sedative she used to knock me out?"

"Not quite," Cain murmured and gestured at the master Glipglow, who in turn snapped their lower jaws in a disapproving response.

"The bacteria were present in the bioreadings we took aboard the *Starshine*—an unknown and unclaimed specimen."

I frowned and rubbed my forehead. "I'm confused. So, Mrs. Gol poisoned me on the *Starshine*? I thought you'd figured that out. I mean, the antidote and everything you whipped up."

"Two separate issues," Cain said.

The master nodded. "Yes. You were subjected to a Class A, subset 29J poison, of which we cleansed you. These bacteria are something else. Something we have not seen before."

"But if the bacteria was in my system…" I trailed off, my mind furiously digging through my memories of every interaction with Mrs. Gol. "Jupiter's stars." I turned and stared at Cain. "That crazy old bat must have put bacteria in the TricLath pudding."

He gave me a blank look.

I rolled my eyes. "I thought she was just being overly friendly and needed a companion or some such nonsense. We were eating, and she gave me her TricLath pudding." To say I felt like a fool would be putting the whole thing mildly. But I was a fool who'd tripped down a ladder and landed in a refuse heap of recycling waste.

My attention swung back to the master. "But how am I still alive? The bacteria"—I brushed past the knowledge of how it'd been introduced into our part of the universe—"is deadly. Everyone infected with it dies. There isn't a cure."

The Glipglow tilted its head. "They did not have us."

Simple yet true. Egotistical or not, the master had been able to unravel the bacteria's mystery when no human medical genius had been able to. Considering Mrs. Gol and her ilk could've continued their nefarious scheming if they weren't so consumed by purist ideology, I felt a little bit of hubris in the master's method of solving the conundrum.

"So you're here because of the bacteria?"

A hatchling climbed up on the master's shoulder and tucked itself into the crook of its neck. The master reached up and gave their youngling a quick scratch of affection. "When we detected the unidentifiable bacteria in your bioscan, we immediately ran it through the Consortium Library Reference DataLogs. This bacterium was not registered, nor were there any pending claims pertaining to any potential variations, natural or synthetic. We staked our claim."

"You staked your claim?"

"It is the right of any master. You carry the only known sample of this bacteria."

"The captain would have had no choice but to turn around at a master's request," Cain clarified. "Turns out if we'd been delayed too much longer or if the *Starshine* hadn't returned when it did, you would be dead." A touch of unexpected concern in his voice caused me to shiver.

"Yes. The bacteria are engineered to work on a specific timetable, gradually and insidiously wreaking damage within a human body," the Glipglow stated.

I looked down at the blanket covering my legs. The bacteria were engineered? What had the hologram officer said? Something about salvaged Eeri bodies. If that was the case, this wasn't a simple issue of introducing a microbe from a new biome where it could cause damage. It meant Pops or the Eeri or whoever had taken the time to genetically engineer these bacteria with a very specific purpose in mind.

My stomach flip-flopped. I leaned over the side of the bed and threw up.

The Glipglow went into action. One hand forced me to lie down while the other took a fresh bioscan. "All systems are back to normal. We don't see any residual bacteria or its effects."

I tried to swat at the Glipglow and its well-meaning intentions. "It's not that. I think it's just—"

"The last several hours have been extremely taxing. She should probably rest for a bit." Cain stepped up next to me and handed me a wipe.

The Glipglow didn't like that explanation. Its lower jaw opened and closed while dripping a fair amount of saliva onto my blanket. "Perhaps. But we will continue to monitor just in case."

The master moved over to one of the *Starshine*'s medical bay workstations and stared at the human technician until they jumped up and got out of the way.

"I'm sorry. I didn't mean to throw up," I mumbled to Cain.

"I meant what I said."

I turned my head to stare at him. "How much do you know?"

When he continued to look everywhere but at me, I knew. Disgust turned sour in my mouth, and I turned my head to watch the master work. I should've known—Cain's reaction was the same with everyone I met who figured out who I was. He'd been nice to me while we were on board the *Rapscallion*, but all that was for show. All he'd cared about was keeping me alive to boost his ratings.

"Case closed, then," I muttered.

My body tensed as his fingers brushed against my arm.

"No," was his soft reply. "There's still the matter of who poisoned you the first time." He paused and corrected himself. "The second time."

"They didn't try again. Your whole bait idea didn't work."

Cain didn't reply.

The master Glipglow stood and returned to the side of my bed. "We can't find anything wrong. Your body is clear of any poison or toxins or bacteria."

Clenching my jaw and abruptly needing to be any-where but there, I swept back the blanket, pushed myself up, and got out of the bed.

"You should rest," the Glipglow stated.

"Thank you for all you've done. I mean it when I say I'm in your debt. If you ever need something, please let me know, and I'll do my best to try to help." But I didn't stick around for any other protests. My jumpsuit, or at least a fresh replacement for my jumpsuit, was neatly folded on the chair next to the bed. I slipped it on, zipped up, and marched out of medical.

When the doors closed, I stopped and leaned up against the wall. I didn't know if the weakness was from having been through the wringer or just from the overwhelming realization of how guilty Pops was. That didn't matter. Everything translated into one undeniable fact: I'd never known who Pops was.

I couldn't stop my thoughts. If I didn't know who Pops was, what did that mean about me? What had been true and what had been a lie? Had he been a xenologist, or had the job been some kind of cover?

Did I want to know? Maybe, for the first time, I truly didn't want to find the answers to those questions. But as much as the revelations hurt, as they fueled a wave of anger toward Pops I'd never experienced before, I knew I would have to find the answers. But first, I needed some food and some peace and quiet to think.

21

At Long Last

The smell of burned circuitry lingered around the Happy Times vending machine as it kicked out a cheeseburger. The maintenance crew must have been overwhelmed. The bun was dry, the meat chewy, and the slice of cheese tasted like plastic. I was tempted to chuck the whole thing in the recycler, but I was hungry. Besides, the buffet table was still a hefty no for me. My little excursion had landed me in medical more times than I'd been in over ten years, and I didn't fancy another round if I could help it.

What in Jupiter's moons was I going to do? The question rolled around in the unsavory bits and pieces of information I'd collected about Pops. I wasn't sure what to feel. The love and admiration I'd carried for him, along with all the times I'd defended him, were tainted.

"Excuse us."

Startled, I turned to see one of the humans on the cruise gesture toward the vending machine. I'd been so lost in my thoughts that I hadn't realized I was blocking his access. Nor had I remembered to chew as I unceremoniously spat some food toward the man while apologizing hastily and stumbling out of the way.

Chewing and swallowing, I wandered through the *Starshine* until I ended up on the observation deck. The space was deserted. Perfect. I took a seat along with the last bite of the cheeseburger and stared out into the vast darkness of space.

Truth be told, I didn't know what to do. Would the time, effort, and emotional toll be worth it to figure out what exactly Pops had been wrapped up in? Honestly, I wasn't sure I wanted to.

A long sigh escaped, and the tears began. My head dropped into my hands, and for a time, I let myself cry, something I hadn't allowed myself to do in quite some time. Pops had always said crying was cleansing, something good for the soul. But over the year spent in IGJ meetings and interrogations, I'd learned tears were weakness, something to exploit.

Pounding footfalls across the floor forced me to look up. I tensed as the sound got closer, and I wished I still had the XS-52. But with a burst of laughter, the two kids from the human family streaked into the observation deck, laughing and shoving each other around.

Counting down from thirty, I scowled. Parents shouldn't let their kids run amok. Annoying little suckers.

I leaned back in the chair as the kids goofed off. They hunkered down on the opposite side and furtively looked at something they'd no doubt stolen. Numerous times, my brother and I had done the same thing—swiped something of Pops's or from one of his work sites, believing the artifact or tool had some hidden magical properties or some such nonsense. A few times, we'd gotten caught. Once, we were even thrown in jail. That was a night I would never forget.

The memories stirred up another question I didn't want to acknowledge. Should I find my brother and let him know? He'd left before Pops had been arrested, and our last conversation was worthy of any jute-store soap story. No, I decided. He was my brother only in memory.

The kids sprang up and ran out of the room. Good. All I wanted was some peace and quiet.

Space was a vast place, full of mysteries and horrors. Even though I'd grown up exploring a great many places, I still dreamed of traveling amongst the stars. Perhaps I had a dream about carrying on Pops's work in my own unique way. But as I stared out the view-field, all I wanted to do was return to my humble apartment and hunker down under a blanket, just to hide from it all.

I balled up the cheeseburger's wrapper and tossed it into a recycler. The temptation to be upset about ever having redeemed the vacation voucher lingered. If I hadn't, I would never have known the truth or at least questioned what I'd been led to believe was the truth.

But as I stayed with the thought, I realized I wasn't upset but simply in shock from everything that'd happened. I was uncomfortable and unsure, but a part of me was glad—glad Mrs. Gol had put her party-planning skills to good use and done what she did. Maybe I wasn't glad about the whole poisoning thing or how she wanted me dead. But she'd exposed me to something that needed to be figured out.

And I would.

"We will."

I didn't turn around. "This has nothing to do with you." *<And quit following me.>*

Cain, in typical fashion, didn't respond but simply moved to stand by my side.

I took a deep breath and slowly exhaled. Who did he think he was?

"Someone who can help."

That made me turn and face him. I jabbed a finger into his chest. "I didn't ask for your help, and I don't need it."

Glittering with flecks of emerald, his eyes flicked up to look past me.

As I was about to chew him out for ignoring me yet again, his arm swept up and shoved me to the ground. As the impact sent explosions of pain through my hip, knee, and wrists, I was ready to let loose a stream of consciousness on exactly what I thought of his help. But my beautiful tirade was interrupted by a very audible pop and a hiss.

I knew that sound. It wasn't gunfire. It was tech, and it was malfunctioning.

As I twisted around, tendrils of smoke were curling out from under the view-field's control panel. Well… Jupiter.

"Get out of here," he hissed as he lifted his weapon.

I ignored Cain, dusted myself off, and walked over to the panel. This was my specialty.

The smoke indicated fire, and fire generated heat. Pulling my jumpsuit's sleeves down to protect my hands somewhat, I found the two release latches. Heat moved through the jumpsuit's material with ease, and as the panel popped off and clattered to the floor, I sucked in a breath and waved my hands a few times from the sting.

Sparks jumped back and forth in the twisted nest of wires and conduits. "I need a suppression canister!" I hollered out to anyone who might've been listening.

Imagine my surprise when one of the human kids ran up to my side with the orange emergency canister. I turned and threw the boy a smile, "Good job, kid. Thanks."

The boy smiled. But not in a way that said, *"Gosh, I'm so glad I was able to help. Look at me! I'm a hero!"* His smile was that of a cat who'd caught a mouse. He raised the canister, and thanks to the lessons I'd learned about not trusting old ladies, I ducked as he threw it at my face.

Note to self: add "Don't trust little kids either" to the list.

"Everyone stay where you are."

Cain wasn't the one issuing the commands but the boy's sister. At least, I'd presumed they were siblings. How silly of me.

The girl held a Mad Mac's disrupter, black market tech. I wasn't great about keeping up with the plethora of weapons being developed and distributed through legitimate channels, much less those on the black market, but when a weapon bore the grinning, cigar-eating face of the guy who'd invented the thing, that certainly made it a lot easier. All about marketing, I guess, as long as the potential customer lived through their encounter with a Mad Mac's weapon to in turn buy their own.

The grin turned into a sneer on the boy's face as he

readied himself for another blow. Ready for it, I caught the canister, gripped the bottom, and tried to twist it back and forth, but the boy was stronger than appearances might suggest. You would think I would've learned not to judge a book by its cover. So sue me. Wait, scratch that—please don't.

My grip slipped as he deftly changed tactics, shoving the canister toward me to throw me off balance and abruptly yanking it back. As I toppled back, out of the corner of my eye, I caught sight of Cain flying through the air toward the boy. The man held a look of feral rage in his eyes as he slammed into the boy, and they crashed to the ground. The canister fell and slid to a stop in front of me.

I reached out to snag the errant canister and thought I could still use it to douse the fire and then smack the little brat, but a blast from the girl's disrupter tore through the flooring a few centimeters from my outstretched fingers, carving a significant hole in the floor. I would hazard a guess that ChowHo Insurance wasn't going to cover that.

"I said don't move."

I didn't. I liked my fingers and other body parts.

"You've had your fun." The girl sighed as if she was bored. Who could've been bored at a time like that?

"He got in our way," the boy growled then threw a hefty punch that hit Cain square in the gut. "We would be off this bucket of bolts by now if it wasn't for him."

A question moved from my mind to the tip of my tongue, but I answered it for myself and instead blurted out the answer to my question. "For crying out loud, you're the assassins?"

"Score one for the lady." The boy's words dripped with sarcasm as he spun in the air and landed another blow to the side of Cain's knee, which dropped him to the ground. With lightning speed, the boy pounced and planted his foot on Cain's neck.

For once, I didn't laugh, especially considering a little boy had bested a grown man. Obviously, the kid had quality bioupgrades, highly likely military grade.

"If he and those annoying Glips hadn't gotten involved, the contract would be closed, and we'd be out of these miserable skins."

I raised my eyebrows. They weren't average assassins, not that an assassin is ever average. This was Tretoono Club–level work, the elite of the elite and one of three groups who used skins. I'd learned something from watching all those true-crime documentaries.

Skinning was a dangerous process for multiple reasons. The biggest concern was the whole setup process, integrating a host of tech and bioupgrades into the brain and central nervous system. Another problem was finding or, better, growing suitable skins or host bodies that wouldn't degrade after a few days. The transfer process was the next problem, moving the consciousness from one body to the other. Even Confore banned the tech, citing too many problems in degradation during each transfer.

"The contract wouldn't have specified any particular reasons why someone wanted me dead, would it?" I asked hopefully.

The girl smiled. "Of course not."

"Could you at least do me the courtesy of telling me who wanted me dead? I mean, I'm going to die anyway, right?"

The boy shrugged and looked at his sister, partner, whatever they were. She nodded.

"Confore," he said.

"Switching on mag-locks," the girl said. She reached down with her free hand, never taking her eyes off us, and punched a button at the top of her boots. A little red light flicked on, blinked twice, and turned green. The boy did the same.

Not good. I figured out what they were doing, and from the continued pops and smoke billowing out from the view-field's control panel, it would be done soon. Those blasted kid-looking things must've planted something when they'd zipped through, pretending to be all innocent and doe-eyed little monsters.

"I have to say using kids as a cover is quite smart."

<*Really, compliments?*>

His snide comment brought only a brief flutter of pain at the base of my skull, which I ignored.

The girl shrugged. "Just a means to an end."

"Ya, your end." The boy snickered.

Another loud pop was accompanied by a long fizzle, followed by a second then a third. The view-field's layers were failing. Whatever those two had planted to eat through wiring and conduits was working rapidly. In a few seconds, it would eat through the tertiary back-ups—not long, ten seconds at most.

Ten…

The boy still had Cain pinned to the floor. If I stretched out a hand, I could probably touch the tips of his boots. That wouldn't do me any good.

Nine…

Eight…

My eyes swung back to the canister then to the hole in the floor. They darted back to Cain.

Seven…

<On my mark, use your tail and grab hold.>

I got a grunt as his body twitched and his tail slid out from underneath him.

Six…

Five…

If I moved a second too soon, the girl would shoot me, which would be messy and hard to explain. I understood why they were waiting. A view-field failure could be explained on a ship like the *Starshine*. Doing so might take a few bribes in the right pockets, but getting away with that would be far easier than explaining why bits of blood and bone coated the observation deck.

Four…

Three…

Two…

<Now!> I screamed in my mind. I lunged for the canister and rammed it into the hole in the floor as the boy lifted his foot off Cain's neck. Cain's tail reached out, encircled my arm, and pulled him toward me as I wrapped my arms around the thick canister and hooked my fingers through the handle. As the control panel lit up like an old-time Reunification fireworks display, Cain wrapped his arms around my waist.

When all the fields failed, the system would trigger the bay door to slam shut. But in the seconds necessary for the signals to move through the system, anything and everything not secured would be sucked into space.

The last field failed, and the abrupt change in pressure ripped through the room, alarms blaring as I held on for dear life.

<Hold on. You can do this.>

<Thanks,> I sent back, not sure I could. You can never appreciate the force of something like that until you've felt as if the universe was trying to suck you up like a piece of dirt off its floor. Time slowed, and I felt every millimeter of skin that rubbed against the smooth, metallic surface of the canister as I slipped.

After what seemed like an eternity, the bay door slammed shut, and I let out a whoop of excitement—short-lived excitement, at least.

"Fine, we'll do this the old-fashioned way," the girl said.

I looked down at Cain, who was crouched low, lips pulled back in a snarl, his canines exposed. To my shock, his eyes had turned black. How many colors were there? I needed a diagram if he was going to keep switching his eye color.

The boy released his mag-locks and aimed a kick at Cain's head. I cringed at the sickening crunch and the subsequent sight of Cain lying on the floor, dazed.

"Come on, Toby, now how we going to move him?"

The boy shrugged. "Shoot 'em and be done with it."

"Really? And how does that get explained?"

Toby shrugged. "No one cares about her, and he's

been kicked down the can. They're not going to waste credits on an investigation into his death."

<Kicked down the can?>

<Not now.>

<Oh, no, it's happening now.>

I ignored the snicker from the boy-man. *<Are you even a real IGJ agent?>*

<Yes.>

So much turmoil was bubbling over from Cain that I was surprised the other two couldn't hear his thoughts.

<I didn't lie. My supervising commander did flash the assignment. I just happened to be in the right place at the right time to pick it up.> Cain paused.

Cain's coal-black irises lightened to a shimmering emerald. "I need to make rank again," he croaked.

"Ya, but don't make you special, does it?" Toby snorted.

"Enough. As scintillating as this is, truly, we're wasting time. Toby, help him up." The girl waved the disrupter at me. "You, get up."

Oh, how I didn't want to comply, but even more, I wanted to march over to Cain and give him a good swift kick of my own. But I did—get up, I mean. The swift kick would have to wait.

"Check it," the girl ordered.

Toby let go of Cain and ran out into the corridor, leaving him swaying but standing. "Clear."

"All right. Let's go."

Toby led the way, and Mad Mac was pointed at our backs. We had no alternative but to go with them. I knew where we were headed. "Old school" meant an airlock, a good old-fashioned disappearing act. That had lost popularity as computers and AI systems improved and erasing video and diagnostic records got harder. Members of the Tretoono Club would have ways to work around the system or enough credits to bribe the entire ship.

<I needed a way to radically boost rank.>

At first, I scoffed and chose to ignore his annoying little voice rattling around in my head.

<I worked all the cases tossed my way, and my rank hasn't moved.>

<Cry me a river.>

<I…>

Even through the telepathy, I heard the hitch, the depth of emotion behind what he was about to say.

<My sister's in jail. Has been for over five years. If I can get my rank boosted back to where it should be, maybe I could open up her case.>

I stopped and turned to face him. "Truth?"

Cain nodded and looked away.

"Come on. Quit playing." The girl poked Cain in the back with the disrupter.

We resumed our death march in silence for a few more moments until we reached one of the airlocks. It was small and out of the way, probably a staff docking entrance.

The girl moved around us and handed the disrupter to Toby. I eyed him as he gave us a devilish grin, but I noted the girl was the one doing all the heavy lifting with the controls. She was obviously the brains of the two.

The inner door opened.

"All right. Get in," the girl ordered.

My mind scrambled for some way out, but I couldn't think of anything helpful. Screaming for help would probably do very little, and Toby would shoot me. Rushing them wouldn't do much good either, not with the enhancements sported by the man-boy and probably her too.

Obviously, Cain didn't share my analysis.

He shoved me hard, tipping me over into the girl, while Cain pounced on Toby. Despite the annoying lack of communication in this plan, I didn't waste the opportunity. I swung with all the force I could muster and landed a blow against the girl's left ear. In an out-and-out physical fight, I could never win. I consider myself in relatively good shape but not fighting shape. The only way I was going to come out on top was to go for where she was most likely vulnerable.

Thanks, help desk job.

A common complaint among bioupgrade users was concussive hits or noises messing with their inner-ear implants. I would be a fool to think an assassin of her caliber didn't have some kind of upgrade there.

Without waiting, I hit her again and then a third time. Her face contorted in pain, and a high-pitched noise began to compete for dominance against the backdrop of fighting.

"You—" Her next word was drowned out by the sound of disrupter fire, and we froze as the blast narrowly missed both of us.

My brief moment of victory didn't last. The girl scrambled out from under me and went on the attack.

Despite her short stature, her blows and kicks were all over the place. I was able to land a few more punches, but the little gremlin was fast, unnaturally fast.

A well-placed kick to my knee forced me back up against the wall. Pain blossomed and radiated up and down my leg. With another blow like that, I wouldn't be able to walk at all. Sensing I was done for, the girl turned her attention to her partner and Cain.

Wrong move, sister. She'd taken her attention off me when I was right next to the airlock control panel. My idea was a gamble, but it was the only shot we had.

<*Get them over toward the door, and when I say, shove the little suckers in.*>

A grunt and a few unkind words were thrown my way, but as I watched, Cain managed to maneuver the fight over in front of the door. I sucked in a deep breath, and my heart raced as he lined them up perfectly. The girl and boy exchanged a look of pure delight as they braced for the final attack.

"Now!" I shouted.

They launched themselves toward Cain, who fell flat to the floor, rolled forward, and sprang up in time to push the two startled assassins into the airlock.

I went to work on the controls, and the inner door snapped shut without hesitation, locked, and started its countdown. The girl looked panicked but tore at the control panel on the other side. Toby snarled and punched the door. It was a heart-pounding, heart-attack-inducing twenty seconds as the girl tried to pry off the panel and fiddle with internal circuitry and Toby's fist worked a nice dent in the door.

As I was about to suggest we make a run for it, the light above the door turned red then yellow then green. The two assassins were sucked out into space—rather fitting, I thought, since that had been their plan for us. But despite my sense of relief, I couldn't watch and pressed my forehead against the cool metal of the wall.

"Are you okay?"

I shook my head and mumbled, "Yes. Just dandy. Never killed anyone before this cursed vacation, so… you know."

"I'm sorry."

Warm arms wrapped themselves around me and pulled me close. Oh, how I wanted to struggle against the abrupt show of affection and concern. But I didn't. Instead, I melted into his embrace and, for the second time in less than an hour, let my tears flow. What was I, some kind of waterworks display? Good grief.

22

A Few Answers

"Well, I guess we owe you another favor," I sighed and leaned back on my elbows.

The Master of Dentar snapped their lower jaws in approval. "You two have brought much-needed excitement to our vacation."

The other adult Glipglow in the room turned and puffed up. I felt their vibrations through the lounge. The master stomped a foot and shot a short sequence of vibrations back. I didn't need a linguist to understand that little conversation.

My hope was that the excitement was over. After I'd sobbed a huge soggy mess on Cain's chest, he convinced me we shouldn't go to the ship's medical personnel but to the Glipglows, which was sound thinking. Our injuries wouldn't be logged into the system, prompting an endless series of annoying questions. I asked about the ship's logs and security feed. Someone would notice the unauthorized use of the airlock and what'd happened. Cain shrugged and cryptically replied that he would see to it.

Did I believe him? I wasn't sure. I did let him escort me to the Glipglows' far roomier hab-unit. They had obviously shelled out a planet's weight of credits for a three-room accommodation. I didn't complain, mind you.

The master had taken one look, ushered us inside, and gleefully assessed the damage. Cain had insisted the master tend to my injuries first while he and the other adult Glipglow slipped out of the hab-unit. The most annoying bit was that Cain ignored the round of questions I threw at him mentally. Typical.

While Cain was gone, I took a chance to ask if the master had learned anything about the bacteria.

"We are running the tests we can. We won't be able to uncover more information until we're back at the nest and can access our equipment. But a first-level theory tilts us to believe these bacteria were genetically altered outside of any currently known practices."

I stiffened as I listened. The idea fit in with what I'd suspected. Pops and the Eeri had worked together. While the Eeri were trading partners for several generations on a variety of goods, they'd been reticent to allow anyone to delve too deeply into their own technology.

"If you're able to find anything else out, will you let me know?"

The Master nodded and began repairing my blown knee.

"Put it on my tab," I sighed.

The door's chime sounded, and Cain stumbled inside to collapse on another of the lounges as the Glipglow sauntered in behind him.

"You need medical attention," the Glipglow told Cain.

He growled, and his tail twitched back and forth.

"Where have you been?" I blurted.

"Those two kids weren't here on their own."

Oh, right. I should've thought of that. I did see them with two adult humans most of the time. "Assassins too?"

"No, handlers."

The Glipglow who'd gone with Cain snapped their lower jaws together a few times. "They've been dealt with."

More than enough information for me.

"You need to rest for the next twenty-four hours. Allow the nanodocs to do their work and repair the damage," the Master instructed as it moved off to inspect Cain.

"This isn't over," Cain tossed out into the room.

I sighed. "I know. The IGJ will undoubtedly have a heap of questions over everything that happened."

I sensed his hesitation.

"What?" I asked.

"When I alerted the IGJ, I expected... annoyance or some kind of dressing down for the undoubtedly complicated situation I was handing them. But the agent I briefed grew nervous, and I was transferred to a chief constable. I repeated my report and was told if they had further questions, someone would be in touch."

"A cover-up," I muttered.

That made sense. Whoever was ultimately in charge of what had happened in the *Rapscallion* obviously had the authority to bury it. The question was whether they would deem it necessary to bury us. Great. Here we go again.

"Yes. But I wasn't initially referring to Mrs. Gol or the IGJ."

"What then?" I asked.

"Confore. When no one reports in to close the contract, they'll send out a new one."

"Thanks for reminding me of that nifty little detail."

"But we could take the fight to them."

I felt a bout of irritation arising. "You keep insisting on this 'we' idea."

"I still need a win, something to boost my ranking."

And there it was—the rub. Even though Cain had shown moments of genuine concern, I was still a tool, something he could use for his own gain.

<It's not like that. At least, it isn't now.>

<Really? I don't recall any great moment of clarity where we bonded, you know,> I slung back at him.

I thought he would fire back, but he didn't. When I glanced over, Cain turned his head away.

Having an ally wouldn't be a bad thing. I reluctantly toyed with the thought. At least he was being up front with his motives. Would it hurt to work with him?

No, it wouldn't. I knew it wouldn't but didn't want to admit that having help would be nice. I also considered the pesky little detail about his supposed sister. If she existed and was truly in trouble, I sympathized with Cain's actions.

"You must rest as well." The master rattled off a few more instructions for Cain.

Sometimes, having bioupgrades wasn't an advantage, not when their damage could wreak internal damage even worse than a few bumps and bruises. He would have to suffer through two more rounds of the Glipglows' specialized nanodocs.

"You will both stay here."

"Oh, no, that's not necessary—" I began.

The master turned their eye on me, and I snapped my mouth shut. To refuse the hospitality of a Glipglow wasn't polite.

When Cain and I were alone, the silence and comfort of being safe wrapped around us. Soon, we both drifted off into much-needed sleep.

My dreams were a wild mixture of events from the past few days, and more than once, I woke up in a cold sweat. The worst had been the image of being laid out on one of the medical slabs with Pops standing there, watching me die.

The first time I woke up like that, I discovered Cain had moved and come to lie down on the other end of the lounge I was using. The second time, I awoke to find I'd scooted closer to him and reached out for his hand.

The third and final time, I woke to find him awake and watching me.

"Creep," I muttered.

"What do you know of Darquets?"

"Taking a page out of Mrs. Gol's book with this line of questioning?"

Cain rolled his eyes.

I sighed and pushed myself up to sit next to him. "Not much. Just low-end gossip."

My hair was a tangled mess, so I started to comb through it with my fingers. "Pops petitioned to do some work on Dar, if I remember correctly. But the government rejected his bid. I don't remember the details, only that he moped around for a few days afterward."

"The Ruling Council is wary of outsiders, especially after the Great Upheaval."

I frowned. "I don't recall hearing about that."

"It's long and complicated but boils down to this," Cain said. "After a long period of growing accustomed to intermingling and open trade with other species, the Ruling Council grew afraid of retaliation with the rise of the purists and the Gene Wars."

I was aware of that. Not all species were biologically compatible, able to produce offspring. Darquets and humans were. It'd been a popular pairing several generations back.

"Where once the Darquets readily shared their technology, goods, and culture with open arms, they closed the planet and learned how to survive on their own. The majority of trade routes were stopped, contracts broken, and travel to Dar limited. They felt the shift in attitudes throughout the galactic community was enough to warrant such drastic measures."

"Have you ever been there? To Dar?"

His sorrow and anger were palpable at the question.

"No. Due to my family's bloodlines, my grandparents weren't allowed to return."

"Seems like they sported some of the same attitudes they feared," I murmured.

Cain shrugged. "Perhaps. But the limitations on who

could return to Dar meant my family was cut off from their heart stones."

"Heart stones?"

After a drawn-out pause, he shifted, turning his upper body toward mine. "Few outside of Dar know about this. Even before the shift in attitudes, this information was considered extremely private."

"Why are you telling me this?"

"So you understand."

I pursed my lips but stayed quiet.

"My sister's genetics are a throwback, and she looks almost full-blooded Darquet. Our father was deathly ill, and no amount of credits or medical intelligence was able to help. He needed the heart stone of our family. Without consulting anyone, my sister hid on a ship bound for Dar, one of the few left allowed to export and import trade goods. She was able to get planetside."

"But she got caught," I interjected.

Cain nodded. "Charged with breaking a myriad of laws associated with unauthorized access to Dar, but the worst was the charge of destroying our family's heart stone. Normally, the Ruling Council handles their affairs internally, but…"

I waited. Confessions of that nature shouldn't be rushed. If anyone could understand that, I could.

As I waited for him to continue, I shuffled through what little I recalled of Dar. The majority wasn't stuff I would repeat, gossip sprung from late-night entertainment, which eventually seeped into those jute-store stories. When Pops petitioned to do research on Dar, I vaguely remembered listening to a few lectures about the planet and its history, enough to orient my brother and me to the culture and language.

The memory sharpened, and I remembered feeling excited as Pops described the planet, probably due to the fact we'd been on Selarious for well over a year, and I was tired of a world dominated by sand dunes. Dar had sounded like paradise, with lush forests, a well-maintained ecosystem full of breathtaking scenery, and a temperate climate where Pops had hoped to work.

Some cautions had been thrown in here and there, something about the formality of its culture or some such stuff. I didn't remember much—too dry and boring for a kid.

Cain cleared his throat. "My mother is Chancellor Heron."

"Huh," I said, borrowing from Cain's vocabulary. That was a revelation I hadn't seen coming. I wasn't sure what to follow it up with, either.

Chancellor Heron oversaw the Aligned Worlds, a loose coalition of governments in charge of mediating conflicts between member worlds. In some circles, they were considered a joke, a token group to make others feel secure when no assurance of security existed. Yet I had read enough to know their negotiations had calmed down several heated situations and, in a couple of incidents, prevented war from breaking out.

"My sister's situation was embarrassing and a dishonor," Cain said with strong dislike.

"And so she had no choice but to turn her over to the IGJ?"

"No. But she did."

"Why didn't she petition Dar for your family's heart stone? As chancellor, she'd have the power and authority to do so."

"As Dar had turned their backs on my family and so many others like us, she turned her back on them."

"And subsequently your sister." I realized how complicated Cain's family truly was.

"Yes."

I pushed myself off the lounge and moved to the small window, another luxury that undoubtedly had set the Glipglows back a hefty sum of credits.

So many family revelations in a short span of time—everything made sense, though. It even explained his excellent taste in clothing.

While our situations were vastly different, they were similar at the same time. We both had family members we wanted to rescue. Cain hoped to find justice for his sister, and I needed to figure out the truth of what Pops was and what had transpired so that no one could ever use it against me.

My decision made, as crazy and stupid as it was, I felt sure of my next few steps.

The door's chime sounded, interrupting my thoughts. My body froze, and I wondered who was there.

Cain sprang into action. His weapon ready, he moved to the side of the door as the master's companion came out of their rooms to answer the door. I caught the shared look of understanding pass between the two of them as the Glipglow opened the door and jumped back.

Cain sprang forward, weapon pointing down into the face of a terrified young human woman.

"I… I have a message to deliver," she stuttered while her body trembled at the sight of Cain and the weapon.

"And what of it?" Cain snapped.

"It's for a Mahia Orion. She wasn't in her hab-unit, and the ship's system noted she was here." The woman extended her hand, which clutched a small parcel. "Please, I'm just doing my job."

Cain pulled back his weapon and snatched the parcel out of her hand. "Get out of here."

The woman threw one last terrified look into the room, turned, and ran. I couldn't blame her. We were on a cruise ship, after all, not in some backwater world's gangster-riddled hotel.

When the door closed, I walked over to Cain. He stepped away from me.

"Hey, that's mine," I said, trying to snag the parcel from him.

"And after what has happened, you think it's wise to open it without precautions?"

I pouted, knowing he was right. But I didn't get packages or correspondence very often. Anything I did get was usually from my lawyers, and the majority of that wasn't fun at all.

"Master of Dentar?" Cain called.

The Glipglow lumbered out of another room and eyed what Cain was holding.

"Do you have a way to scan this?"

Without further ado, the Master reached out and ran a claw along the length of the parcel. They let out a series of incomprehensible sounds, and the other Glipglow ran their talon over the parcel. The two consulted.

"Well?" I couldn't contain my impatience.

"We detect no biochemical concerns, and our nest-mate detects no other threats."

"Satisfied?"

Cain shrugged and tossed me the parcel.

I caught it and scowled at him. "What if it's some priceless artifact and I didn't catch it?"

He shrugged again and sat back down on a lounge.

The parcel was wrapped in brown paper, a luxury item. I didn't know anyone wealthy enough to afford to waste a piece of paper like that. Then again, I hardly knew anyone at all. With care and more than a bit of excitement, I pulled back the paper to reveal a small t-square.

My shoulders slumped forward. "Great."

Cain tensed, his hand moving to his holstered weapon. "What is it?"

"Another stupid cryptic message. You know, I thought you'd sent me that first one. Trying to be all secret IGJ agent and junk."

"I didn't send it," he frowned.

"Yes, I know. It was the Star Eaters."

Cain stood. "What? Why didn't you tell me?"

"Well, we were a little preoccupied at the time, or don't you remember the crazy old woman?"

I was unable to stop Cain from snatching the t-square from my hand and marching over to the Sur-T Screen.

"Hey," I said and stomped after him. An urge reared up as I eyeballed his tail. Unfortunately, he sensed what I wanted to do and pulled his tail out of the way. *<Spoilsport.>*

He plugged in the t-square, and the screen's logo switched from the Desmo Voro Starshine Adventures to the logo of Bloodhearst & Strobe.

"Isn't that your lawyer?"

"Yes." I nodded, not having a good feeling about what might be on the t-square. "Someone must have already gotten wind of our little misadventures and started a lawsuit. The office had a stellar reputation for rapid response times."

The logo disappeared, and the image of none other than Harrison Bloodhearst appeared on the screen. I was shocked. No one had seen the elder Bloodhearst in years. Rumors had him holed up on Old Earth in some over-the-top castle reconstruction. If he was still alive, that was only thanks to his being able to afford ample life extensions, which I helped fund, no doubt.

"Mahia Eimariana Orion, this message was left by your father, Wats Hawking Orion, to be released upon the communication between the austere offices of Bloodhearst and Strobe and the Celestial Light."

I nearly fainted and would have if not for Cain reaching out to steady me.

"You are instructed to pay an in-person visit to Bloodhearst and Strobe's satellite office on Cleary Station at your earliest convenience. I am not allowed to specify details or clarify any questions or concerns you may have, due to the insecure nature of this communication. If you wish to speak to a representative, please do so upon your visit to our satellite office on Cleary Station."

Mr. Bloodhearst's image vanished, and the t-square popped out of its port.

"Celestial Light?" Cain asked.

I stumbled over to one of the lounges—heavenly days, a lot of them were crammed into that room—and plopped down.

At least the communique answered one question: whether the Star Eaters had been lying about knowing Pops.

"Celestial Light." Cain growled. That wasn't a question but a demand for answers.

I looked up at Cain. "The Star Eaters."

He narrowed his eyes and knelt in front of me. "What do those things have to do with this? Besides the obvious, mysteriously whisking you out of Mrs. Gol's way?"

"I'm not sure. But they knew Pops." I wanted to tell him the whole story, but my mind locked itself down, and I stood, needing to pace back and forth to expel the building tension.

Why shouldn't I share what had happened with him? Cain had opened up about his family. But I couldn't, not yet. Perhaps my revelations were still too raw, too unsettling. I needed more information before I began to speculate widely with someone else about what Pops had been caught up in.

Cain stood and crossed his arms, his tail madly twitching back and forth. "I suppose this means you're off to Cleary Station."

Did it? No timetable had been specified, only the polite phrase "at your earliest convenience."

"No." I slipped back toward my earlier decision. The

message from my lawyers added a new dimension to the whole mess. And to be honest, I wasn't ready for more earth-shattering revelations. I had plenty to unpack and digest without adding more to the unsettling mystery that was my pops.

I turned to face Cain. "No. First, we figure out why Confore thinks I'm tied up with Jorge. Figure out what this Project Clear Sight business is. You solve the case and move up in your ratings. Then I'll go to the station and sort through my mess."

A spark of amber shone in his eyes for a moment before they returned to their vivid violet shade. "When the *Starshine* stops at its next destination, we'll grab different transport out."

"Yup, and head home. Or at least my home." Back to the Original Luna, where I'd spent the last few years, to the overcrowded cities of out-of-luck humans and tourists eager to get as close as possible to Old Earth.

"No."

I frowned. "What?"

"First, we head to Lunar 5, where Jorge was last at. We start there and work our way back to the Original Luna."

All right. I followed that line of reasoning: work on the periphery first, gather information, then strike at the heart of the puzzle.

"Promise me something," I asked.

Cain nodded.

"Just don't use me as bait again, okay?"

To my shock and delight, Cain actually smiled. "Can't promise that."

Thank you for reading *The Rapscallion*!

Don't miss out on what happens next for Mahia and Cain or explore what other titles I have to offer. You can sign-up to stay in touch through my newsletter at:

elizabethknollston.com

You can also follow me on social media at:
facebook.com/elizabethknollston
twitter.com/EKnollston

Look for the second installment of the
The Three-Fold Suns Series

Project Clear Sight

and discover the twists and turns that are on the horizon!

Acknowledgements

There are so many people to thank for being a part of making this life long dream come true. First and foremost, the biggest thank you is to my parents who encouraged a love of reading and demonstrated the value of exploring the endless adventures contained with the pages of a book.

I've had so many family and friends who have supported me in this adventure of a life time, I am afraid I would leave too many out if I started naming them. But I have to say a special thank you to the one person, who without her friendship and support as a fellow author, I wouldn't be where I am today. Thank you Naomi for all of you advice, support, and believing in me!

And I would be remise not to say a warm and loving thank you to my aunts and uncles who have become such a special part of my life and didn't hesitate to cheer me on when I took the plunge to make this career official.

Last but certainly not least, because without them this story wouldn't be where it is today, are the editors at Red Adept Editing. I appreciate all of the work which was done in order to help this story shine!

Thank you everyone for encouraging me and believing in me! Thank you readers for taking a chance on this book and I look forward to writing more fantastical and intergalactic adventures!

About the Author

Elizabeth Knollston collects dragons. No, they're not real. But if you know of a mad scientist or genetic engineer who's working on the real deal, be sure to let her know. She would dearly love to collect star ships too, but those won't fit in her garage.

Her (overactive) imagination is credit to her parents, who outrageously encouraged her poor spending habits of buying too many books. And just a side note—if you ever plan on moving, book collecting isn't helpful.

In another life, Elizabeth dreamed of becoming an archaeologist, but a fascinating and rewarding job as a therapeutic horseback riding instructor derailed those plans. When Elizabeth isn't wondering about being on a manned mission to Mars, she enjoys bugging her dog, battling the weeds in her garden, and being a productive member of society.